BOOK 1: THE EXODUS SERIES

Flight from the Water Planet

By Austine Etcheverry
&
D. Jean Quarles

Published by Rocky Mountain Creative Publishers
707 Park St, Alexandria, MN 56308
www.rockymountaincreativepublishers.com
(A division of Rocky Mountain Entertainment)

First published in 2012

The Library of Congress Cataloging-in-Publication Data
is available from the Library of Congress
ISBN 978-1-933868-50-9
Printed in the United States of America

Dedicated to:
Danielle,
Dustin,
Trenton
&
Macen

Flight from the Water Planet

Author's Note:

∞

    Those of Earth are among the few in the galaxy who are not advanced in the use of thought transfer. The alien beings on the following pages use mental communication instead of verbal language. This means that instead of quotations you will find this symbol ∞ to show their thought transfers or dialog. It represents the alien's ability to separate their thoughts into those that are public and those that are private.

March 10th

Chapter 1

Gillian lay sprawled across her bed. She idly tapped her pencil on the book in front of her. Letters. That's all she saw, a bunch of letters. Her mind refused to allow her rest. She had so much to do. She turned her gaze toward her English book. Yeah, that, too. A test or quiz, she couldn't really remember which, only that it would represent a large portion of her grade for the semester. Why was she having so much difficulty concentrating? She sighed and looked back at her history book, only to realize she had to turn back several pages and start over.

Music played, and while most of the time that soothed her, tonight every song was a favorite that had her singing along and wishing she could jump up and dance. Really she wished she could forget about history and English all together. Be like other kids she knew who didn't care about grades or assignments or even tests, for that matter.

Instead she shook her head, as if to shake loose the thoughts that consumed her and once again tried to focus her attention on her book.

A song ended and in the lull between, Gillian thought she heard a noise. She pulled the headphones from her ears, tilted her head and listened. She didn't hear anything for a second and was about to put them back on when a muffled cry rang out. Curious, she rose from her bed. Were her parents really upset with each other? What was going on? She had never heard them shouting before.

The old house they had bought in Jackson, Wyoming had creaking floors, but Gillian had already learned the ins and outs of quiet movement. She was an early riser and many weekend mornings slipped downstairs to make coffee and breakfast for herself before her parents woke. Now she used the same stealthy walk until she got to the top of the stairs. There, Gillian stopped and listened.

"We can't stay." Her mother's voice was clipped and angry. "It's impossible."

"We can't leave either," her father said, quietly, so much so that Gillian had to strain and lean over the banister.

She heard something slam against the counter-top and she startled. What was going on? Then she heard a sob. She could no longer control her curiosity. She needed to know what was happening between her parents.

She descended the stairs quietly, but without care of being heard and rounded the corner to step into the kitchen.

One of the amazing things about her parents was they never fought or yelled at each other. She had loved that about them. Too often she'd been hanging over at friends' homes and heard their parents fighting. It never felt comfortable to her, always awkward. Concern filled her mind. Could her parents be unhappy together? Was this what happened right before a divorce? Gillian's eyes began to water and her lips trembled.

In the kitchen she saw her mother and father as they stood facing each other. Their faces red, and eyes wild, they looked crazy. Never had she seen them this way before. Now

14

her fear of what was happening became even more real. Something was incredibly wrong.

"It makes no difference. We can't run far enough. Maybe it's better that way," her father said. He placed his hands on her mother's shoulders.

"We can try. We can't give up. You never know," her mother argued. "We could be the lucky ones."

Her father's head tilted and he gave her a reproachful look that accompanied the words, "You know what it could mean."

Her mother shook her head as if to shake off his words. "South, we could go south," she argued. Gillian saw her mother step into her father's arms. They weren't upset with each other at all. Gillian stayed perfectly still. They still hadn't noticed her.

"If we stay, we'll die," her mother said.

"I know," he answered.

Gillian wasn't aware she'd gasped until she saw her parents turn.

"Gillian! I thought you were . . ." her mother's voice sounded pained, she looked up to her husband, and then away.

Gillian's father pivoted out of her mother's embrace and came toward her. "Come here," her father said and opened his arms to her.

"You can't," her mother grabbed at his arm. "No! I mean it! No!"

Gillian watched as her father carefully drew her mother's hand away from his arm. "She needs to know," he said, staring into his wife's eyes.

Her mother's hand flew to her mouth. Tears flooded her eyes and ran down her cheeks.

He came toward her, filling her entire vision with his body. His hands rested on her shoulders, the same position he'd just shared with her mother, but now he seemed suddenly without words. "Gillian," her name was strangled from his throat. He shook his head. Behind them she heard her mother sob and then what sounded like her sinking to the floor.

Gillian's eyes widened. She stepped around her father to run towards her mother. Her father stopped her. He took her hands and led her across the room to the kitchen table where he sat her down.

"You're almost an adult. I need to tell you something that may be hard for you to hear. It's something that can never be spoken of outside our home. Never. Do you understand?"

On the floor, her mother keened and rocked back and forth, but she looked up and nodded as if she also realized that Gillian needed to know.

Her father's voice lowered, his tone calmer still, "Gillian, do you understand? You can't speak about this. Ever. To anyone."

"What? What's going on? I don't understand."

"We were sent to Wyoming because of . . . problems," he explained. "With Old Faithful and the other geysers in Yellowstone." Her mother and father were the leading North American thermal experts. "We have had confirmation. We are sure. The Yellowstone volcano is ready to erupt."

Gillian nodded, waiting. There had to be more. What did it mean? Volcano's erupted all the time. There was one in Hawaii that had been erupting for years. Sure Yellowstone's was a super volcano, but . . .

16

"We can't know for sure. We could be safe somewhere else," her mother said.

But Gillian saw in her father's eyes. He was sure no place was safe.

Chapter 2

∞

A host of heavenly bodies floated over the staging area on TE Garon. As their images coalesced, Soluma-Rah gave order to her private thoughts. There was much to be discussed this meeting, yet, in her opinion, only one issue would take precedence - the Water Planet.

She had no way of knowing how those from the Federation of Life Sources would gather her public thoughts. When Soluma-Rah heard the kong, she knew all were in attendance.

Clearing her mind of private thoughts, Soluma opened herself for public thought transmission. ∞-Most High Beings,-∞ she acknowledged. ∞-May your planets all gain health and wholeness. I have read your reports listing the concerns to be discussed in our limited time together. Blessings to you for having submitted them.-∞ Soluma cast her eyes around the area, nodding to each Being's image.

∞-As your Most High Elected, I have set the order of discussion.-∞ She quickly sorted out the minute difficulties faced by the planets under her authority. Docking issues, trade issues and the ever-present issue of planetary space - who had right of way. The holographic images before her were in quiet agreement. No one seemed that concerned over the usual challenges they faced. A new and entirely different problem had come to their attention. It was time to broach the subject.

∞-It seems a vast number of Beings are concerned over the Water Planet in the Snowy Zone.-∞ Soluma heard the public murmurs in her mind. The loudest of those belonged to Bodha. A moderate Being, she acknowledged his right to share thought.

∞-Thank you, Most High,-∞ his thought transfer was seamless and the others quieted. ∞-As esteemed bodies of the Astral Zone, we have set an agreement to not interfere. I know there have been violations of this agreement. However, I believe we should still take no collective action. Those without thought are primitive. They have had much knowledge foolishly given to them.-∞

Soluma-Rah wondered if Bodha now cast his private thoughts to Ka. Bodha had approached her on numerous occasions stating what could not be confirmed, but also could not be denied. Ka traveled toward the Water Planet. Was he also taking something? Sharing thought? Those to whom power belonged in the past had been quick to share thought with those from the Water Planet, but it seemed that still the planet struggled amongst themselves, unable to unify their Beings. Soluma returned her attention to Bodha's thoughts.

∞-Yet, the thoughtless seem unable to join our collective intelligence. I am aware their planet is in danger. Perhaps it is best these thoughtless lose their life force.-∞ Bodha respectfully returned thought to Soluma.

Soluma saw several other Beings in agreement with what Bodha had philosophized. The Water Planet had been given much knowledge in the past, and it had almost led to disaster for the inhabitants many times. Too often they used the knowledge given to spread fear and create conflict with each other. She, too, was disappointed in their use of thought.

Rohongra presented her plea to speak. ∞-Most High Bodha, while I understand your position, I feel as compassionate Beings, we must consider other life forces, even those with lesser communication than our own.-∞

Immediately, others overran Rohongra's thoughts. A disrespectful act that angered Soluma-Rah, but before she could regain control, Ka forced the discussion.

∞-Ha! Rohongra may speak of compassion, but all know her truth. It is the same truth for us. Water Planet's thoughtless can be made to assist us in our endeavors. In two more rotations, we shall no longer be able to gift our fellow Beings with Polisis mineral. We can no longer allow our workers to perish for other's greed.-∞

Polisis mineral shaped and molded into shields protected the Beings of Rohongra's planet from the life taking starshine. Soluma breathed deeply. Without the mineral, those of Rohongra's planet would perish, but also Soluma knew they would be unable to provide power source to the others in the federation. Both Ka and Rohongra had, at other meetings, spoken of the need for workers. The mining and collecting of Polisis, the mineral, and Duji, the power source, meant pain for their planet's Beings.

Ka continued his thoughts, ∞-We have argued long about the challenges the Beings on my planet have struggled with. Yet, at these council meetings, none have brought forth an idea that could be made good. None of you wish to send your Beings to work, and possibly die, on our worlds. The Water Planet bodies can answer our need.-∞

20

∞-Ka, I understand your position. It is honest, if against our principles. I cannot vote to affirm,-∞ Bodha's thoughts interrupted.

Rohongra immediately grabbed the forum. ∞-Most High Bodha, Most High Beings, may I remind you of the cost to you? When Ka is no longer able to present us with Polisis, we will not willingly give Duji. We are aware of the power of Duji, and so have been willing to sacrifice to share it with all of you. That will come abruptly to an end if we do not receive Polisis.-∞

Soluma felt the silencing of the minds as all thoughts turned private. They had kept their treaties for twenty solstice runs. Rohongra's public thoughts frightened them all.

She gave the floor to Ora-J. ∞-Really, Most High Beings, does it matter whether they're harvested for our use or left to die?-∞

Soluma-Rah gaged the thoughts of the others. Her thoughts were drained and she felt the weight of all present. They had dipped into her mind and left something behind - knowledge that was uncomfortable.

They shared more thoughts and finally together they found commonality.

∞-I shall read our agreement.-∞ All thoughts stopped transmitting instantly.

∞-Allowable 1: All Most High Beings are in mutual agreement.

Allowable 2: The Water Planet shall be evacuated. Each planet shall send representatives who shall remove entities for transport.

Allowable 3: As superior Beings, we will be compassionate to those who are removed.

Allowable 4: The use of these entities will be at the discretion of each Most High and Planet.

Allowable 5: Those Most High, who wish, may release their transported entities on neighboring uninhabited planets for life sustaining purposes.-∞

These were the thoughts they could agree on, the thoughts that would allow the federation to continue. Soluma waited to see if there would be any more thought transmissions. Quietly, one by one, the host of heavenly bodies left the staging area.

Soluma-Rah sat tortured in the staging area. ∞-What have we done?-∞ Those who helped with the council meeting scurried around, not interrupting her thoughts, nor opening theirs to her.

Soluma had become Most High Elected when her father left the planet. She was much too young to be in a position of authority, but then, that had been comets ago. Why was it she felt as unsteady now as she had then?

An errant thought intruded, ∞-It's wrong.-∞

Startled, Soluma-Rah gazed at those in the room, trying to discern whose thoughts had come to her. When she realized the source, she felt shame. Her father's thoughts, from that place where no communication comes, jarred her. How could that be? How could she have so clearly heard his words? Soluma blinked rapidly.

One of her planetary Beings saw her and stopped his ministrations, appearing perplexed. She nodded, then rose and fled the room with too many eyes and too much knowing without any wisdom at all.

* * *

Rohongra waited a full ekton longer than necessary to make sure her Being was fully private before she rose and stomped out of the heaven chamber. Outside the starlight beamed down on her planet, causing shimmery waves that took her eyes another ekton to adjust to. While she was the Most High Elected of ThAak-too, she held no illusion she was in charge. No, Dahi, the Supreme Thought Leader, really made the decisions for the bodies of ThAak-too.

It was Dahi who had informed Rohongra she must speak for Ka so her planet could continue to receive Polisis. Rohongra lifted her protective face covering to spit. How had her planet come to this? She still remembered when starlight warmed them and gave them life. Now starlight sucked life from their bodies, causing them to wear mined-metal sheaths to survive. She pounded her way through the crowd of ThAak-toos waiting in alignment for sustenance. Those without sheaths, with nothing to protect them and no one to stand for them, crawled on the planet floor, their outer Beings covered with pus-filled pockets - their moons shortened.

∞-I am waiting,-∞ Dahi thought to her.

Rohongra refused to open her thoughts to him. Instead, she watched while a particularly decrepit ThAak-toon stirred the dust over his body, hoping to cool himself. The ThAak-toon reminded her too much of her brothers. Too much of her father. All removed from the planet forever.

A loud noise interrupted her thoughts. The aligning ThAak-toons gathered around the Being Rohongra had been watching. She was reluctant to see what had happened, yet felt she had no choice but to follow through. As she came closer, those without sheaths quickly scurried out of her way.

23

She looked down at the Being. His life force was ebbing. Rohongra wanted to hold him, to touch him, but that would hurry his life force away. Only those wearing sheaths could touch each other, all others would perish from the contact.

∞-I am waiting,-∞ Dahi thought to her again.

Rohongra looked to the heavens. ∞-I am coming.-∞ Rohongra rose, more determined than ever to champion her plan. Dahi might be the Supreme Thought Leader, but his thoughts had become stale.

She continued her way across the dust and then descended under the surface, relishing the cooler temperature, still hot, but not blistering. When she entered Dahi's private chambers she felt a chill, but it came from Dahi's presence.

∞-I wondered what kept you. I felt your presence coming long ago.-∞ Dahi reclined on mounds of cushions, each feather-light and soft to the touch.

Rohongra waited for her eyes to adjust to the dimness before she responded, and then she refused to give thought to why she was late. ∞-Ka behaved as expected. The Most High Council has agreed to remove the disposables from The Water Planet.-∞

Dahi's guttural snort did nothing but anger Rohongra. ∞-I can see you have less taste for this solution to our problems.-∞

∞-I have no taste for this solution at all.-∞ Rohongra lifted the hood of her sheath from her head.

∞-Starlight is increasing. It gains strength each planet rotation. It beats down on our Beings and sucks life force. Soluma-Rah knows this, Ka knows this, even Bodha must know of this.-∞

24

∞-So you think? Then why do they not come to save our Beings instead of worrying over those of the Water Planet? Why do they not come to take the energy source themselves? No, they know nothing. They think only what we wish them to think.-∞

∞-Our planet no longer wants our Beings. It destroys them. It is time for us to find a new home.-∞

Dahi's eyes crinkled. ∞-Our energy source increases with each rotation. Yes, it creates some problems, but those of us with sheaths can do well. Those without, well, we know why they suffer. It's just they do so.-∞

It seemed horrific to Rohongra the same starlight that was reducing her planet's Beings' life was increasing the power of Duji they were now pulling from the ground.

∞-How can you think it is just? The Beings who have been reflecting on our power have drawn some interesting conclusions. Even you must know they have truth? We shall not survive soon, even with the Polisis sheaths.-∞

Dahi moved his limb across his body, asking for her silence. ∞-You will think no more on it! Leave me!-∞

Rohongra purposefully took longer than necessary to replace the hood on her head. Her thoughts, though closed to Dahi, did not stop.

* * *

On the planet YonYa, Bodha paced. For many rotations his planet had aligned with the council and it had resulted in peace between their worlds. At first, his Beings were reluctant to put down the devices of protection. Many now living had no knowledge of that other time. Bodha seriously wondered what would happen if a break occurred between the council and their planet.

Bodha scanned the scene outside. Calm reigned. He saw the Beings, who placed their wellness in his wisdom, floating about playing. Joy. That was what his planet experienced because of their affiliation with the Most High Council. Joy would be what they would lose if they didn't follow through.

Several mims away, the last of the starships still waited. Once peace came, their Beings had no need of them. Yet Bodha was adamant they could not trust fully those of Celute. Ka had strength and cunning. Those of ThAak-too were also to be feared. They had much power at their disposal.

Bodha composed his thoughts. He worked to calm himself. When he stepped out, the Beings below him turned as one. When all their faces were to him and their minds tuned in, he began. ∞-My desire is complete. My thoughts are one with yours. The council has agreed upon a course of action and we must participate. Entities are in need of our wisdom and relief. Those of the Water Planet in the Snowy Zone are at risk of leaving. While those of the council know they are without much knowledge and thought, the council agrees we should provide salvation.-∞ Bodha lifted his head higher. ∞-We shall set to work immediately to prepare the starships to evacuate as many entities as possible. They are to be relocated within our Heavenly Zone.-∞ Bodha bowed and stepped back out of sight. He closed his thoughts to them and bent low. He prayed they were all not lost.

When he rose, he moved swiftly to the compound where his people were already preparing the ships for travel. He entered the first starship. His first companion, Momur, hurried to his side.

26

"How can this be?" Momur used his voice.

Bodha stood stunned. The Beings surrounding them stared and, when they saw Bodha glance their way, were careful to turn away and resume their work.

∞-You, of all, should know.-∞ Bodha thought.

Momur, realizing his disrespect, bowed and made to leave, but Bodha stopped him. He ordered the others to leave them alone. One by one, Beings slipped away.

∞-I had hoped you would lead us.-∞ Bodha thought when the two were alone.

"How can I? We agreed," Momur's voice, so long, unused was raspy.

They had come too far to return to the other ways. Bodha shook. "If there was any other way, the council would have taken it," he acquiesced and used his voice too.

"Do you remember how our Beings felt when we were invaded for our own good?" Momur swirled around the spaceship, his anger creating waves of energy.

"I know we thought at the time it would be our demise, but see . . ." Bodha stilled his friend.

"I saw more than half of our Beings leave. Not only were they lost, but those of other planets lost many, too. That is what we are faced with. And you, more than any other, know why."

"Ka is a problem. I will grant you that. But the council made the decision as a group. If we are to continue, to be allowed peace, we must follow the others. To show disrespect could mean we would no longer be allowed to participate in the council. We'd be at the mercy of Ka and others like him."

Momur stopped his dreaded swirling movement. "So either way we shall perish."

Bodha soothed his friend's being. "We shall not. We will join with the others in their task. We have been told the evacuees can go wherever we choose to take them. We shall not bring them here. I believe I have already found a suitable home for them. They shall not disrupt our planet."

"I do not trust Ka."

Bodha nodded. "Nor I, my friend. But Soluma-Rah does not trust either. She will protect us all."

∞-I should not have doubted you.-∞

Bodha clouded his thoughts, for he also had concerns he did not wish his friend to know.

* * *

Ka swiftly rose, he was elated at the turn of events. Those of ThAak-too played the game well. Rohongra gave no inkling of the grave danger her Beings were in, but Ka knew and he was pleased. Now his planet would be able to mine more of the mineral Polisis, so precious to ThAak-toons and those Beings of the other planets. While the ThAak-toons wore it for protection, others wore it as a sign of wealth.

He turned when he felt a presence behind him. His precious stood there. Her skin glowed most bright and her robes flowed and sighed as she entered his private realm. ∞-I felt you had concluded. I could wait no longer,-∞ Omis thought.

Ka leaned over and placed his head beside hers. ∞-Yes, I was coming to give you news. The council agreed.-∞

Swiftly Omis's thoughts came to Ka. He let them enter and linger while he remained beside her. ∞-You will now be considered as Most High of Most High. Think how much the

28

Disposables will be able to mine. Imagine! We shall have all the energy source we need. And oh, how our bodies will shine.-∞

Omis moved closer to Ka's Being. ∞-Your offspring will be so proud. When shall you tell the planet?-∞

∞-At half-light I will tell them. Until then, I have much to review. The council does not believe the Disposables fully know of their challenges. They may not be eager to come up the ramps into our transportation discs.-∞

∞-So what shall you do? Wait for the land movements? Won't that decrease the number of beings we can use?-∞

∞-Soluma-Rah has listened to the Disposables thoughts. There are some who know of the crisis. They have not informed the other entities.-∞

∞-Will the movements be abrupt?-∞ No thoughts transferred. ∞-Perhaps a minor land movement would help to convince them they should save as many as they can.-∞

Ka's heart-space opened wide for his precious. ∞-Your thoughts are perfectly aligned with mine.

Soluma-Rah has not made any conditions for the removal of the Disposables. I will inform all and we shall immediately move to prepare the discs for occupancy and travel.-∞

Omis purred. ∞-Soon then, we shall have more of the beings.-∞

March 16th

Chapter 3

The rain came down, huge drops that made pitter-patter sounds on the glass of the Riverton High School windows. A chill caused Johnny's six-foot muscular frame to tremble, but it wasn't because of the cold. It was nerves. He had staked everything on this choice. He'd lost his debate partner and his chance at going to the National Speech and Debate meet because of a girl. Johnny's old debate partner's voice resonated in his brain. The last angry words Johnny heard from Wesley the week before had been of the old saying, "Bros before Hos."

Wesley needed Nationals to attend the college he wanted. His whole life revolved around this. But Johnny was in love, and if that meant doing a poetry piece at the state meet to get her attention, well then, he was all in. Wesley would have to go to state alone and debate for his life. Johnny tried to tell him he would be better off without him, but Wesley didn't see it that way.

"Johnny, it takes weeks to prepare for a good Lincoln-Douglas debate. I've never even debated on my own. You know that."

"Wesley, you'll be fine. Stop fighting it. You don't need me."

"It's not you I need. It's our debate topic, jerk. I worked weeks to get all our information together; I spent hours preparing for this competition. My future depends on going to Nationals. You know it, yet you're going to pick some girl over me. You're shameless. Poetry! Have you lost your mind?"

The slamming of locker doors interrupted Johnny's thoughts. It brought him back to reality. This was his moment. He wiped his sweaty palms on his pants, ran his hand through his black, curly hair and waited for his angel to appear.

Trisha and Victoria came around the corner together. Johnny could hear pieces of their conversation "You ready for the meet this weekend?" Trisha asked Victoria.

"I've been working on new evidence. I really like debating animal rights. I think we might be able to take it all the way. How about you? Any deep poetry piece you're giving to the world this weekend?" Victoria asked.

"Maybe. It's still in the works," Trisha said, pulling out a brand new tube of cherry lip balm and putting a fresh layer on.

Johnny saw Victoria look his way as he lounged by the lockers. "Did you hear the rumor about Johnny and Wesley?" she asked, lowering her voice. He tried to look away and pretend he couldn't hear the conversation. He didn't know if he wanted to get an up close preview of how Trisha would feel when she heard he'd ditched his debate partner.

"What?"

"They aren't debating together this weekend in Casper."

"No way. Why not?" asked Trisha.

"Nobody knows," Victoria said.

Trisha stopped walking as she realized Johnny stood in front of her locker. Victoria quickly looked at her feet.

"Hey, Johnny. Victoria was spreading some rumors about you. She says you and Wesley aren't debating together this weekend?"

Victoria glared at her friend.

Johnny nervously laughed. "No, I'm going to try poetry. I actually stopped by because I wanted to see if you could give me a hand and work out the kinks in my piece?"

"Um, sure I guess," Trisha said. "We have to be on the bus at two. How about I see you then?"

"Sounds good." Johnny headed slowly in the direction of his class, knowing the girls stared after him.

"I think we learned the reason they aren't debating together," he heard Victoria say.

"No way, you're crazy. There has to be some other reason. Poetry is an excuse," Trisha replied. He wondered if her shy smile had crept to her lips.

"Well, you'll have two days to find out. Let's go. We're late for science and you know how Mr. Pierce gets when we're late."

Johnny smiled to himself.

Time ticked slowly as the speech and debate team endured the last class of the week. Two o'clock and they would be free.

Johnny, in Algebra 1, drummed his fingers nervously, while watching Wesley across the room. He sat rigid staring straight ahead. And when the clock finally struck two, all thirty-five of the Riverton speech and debate team members ran out the doors. Johnny noticed their head coach, Mark, waited in front of the school for his team.

Once everyone was present, the coach spoke, "Okay team, this is it. State. The big one! I'm aware you know many of the kids as friends. Some of you have debated with them for years, gone to their homes and maybe even had dinner with their families. But they're your competition this weekend. So team, put your game faces on. Let's do it." The kids roared.

The students were all different shapes and sizes with varying talents, but together they were a team determined to bring home the championship and trophies galore. One by one, with their luggage in tow, they boarded the bus, taking their spots. No freshmen were allowed in the back unless given permission by a senior.

Johnny slowly stepped on and stopped when he saw Wesley in the second seat from the front.

"That's freshman land," he said.

"Move on, Johnny."

"Whatever." Johnny continued until he found what he was seeking. He located her sitting in her seat all alone. He stopped. "Can I sit here?"

Trisha pulled the headphone buds out of her ears. "What?"

"Can I sit?" She nodded with a smile, and to the left, he saw Victoria give her a thumbs-up.

Two days of this and Johnny thought he might stand a chance. When everyone was finally seated, the bus moved ahead. Johnny felt his life going forward.

Chapter 4

"Mandy, get off the phone. We have to go," her brother, Derek, shouted to her.

"Sherry, my brother's screaming about being late. I gotta finish packing. I'll miss you. I can't believe your coach won't let you come."

"I know. What did he think we're going to do in Torrington, Wyoming? Drink coffee and practice our speeches? Get real. We go to rodeos and get rowdy. Oh, well! Win one for me, girl, and tell that fine brother of yours I said hello."

"Heck, yeah, on the first request. Not a chance on the second one." The girls laughed as they hung up. Mandy shoved one more pair of heels into her suitcase, looked at herself in the mirror, pushed a brown lock of hair behind her ear, and rushed out to where her brother waited impatiently.

"Big meet. My chance to get out of this town. Bus leaving without me. Any of this matter to you?" Derek drawled.

Derek had the looks in the family. The best of both parents, blond hair and great skin. It was such a shame he was often a jerk. Still, she loved him.

Mandy handed her suitcase to Derek. His temper tantrum increased as he tried to lift the bag into the back of the truck.

"Mom wants us to stop by the store and say good-bye on our way to school," Mandy said.

Mandy and Derek's parents owned the Shoshoni ice cream shop located at the major crossroads leading to Casper, the nearest shopping mecca for that part of the state. People came from hundreds of miles around to get a cone. It was an embarrassment to Derek, but Mandy thought it was awesome so many people loved her parents' store.

"Call Mom and tell her we don't have time. You took too long."

Mandy pulled out her phone. She twirled her hair around her finger, and sadly broke the news to her mom that Derek felt the need to be at school an hour early in case the weather pushed the bus to leave before planned.

"Mom says to be safe and drive slowly because the roads are getting icy," Mandy told him.

"I will, I will. Love you Mom," he yelled. Mandy said good-bye and hung up.

"I don't know why you have to be so mean," Mandy said.

Derek shook his head and turned up the radio, moving the piece of straw he chewed to the other side of his mouth. Mandy slumped farther in the seat and stared out the window, wondering what life would be like if Derek got his way and left for college next year. Stupid big brothers, she thought.

Mandy decided to focus on something else. She leaned forward and turned down the radio so she could recount the details of her and Sherry's conversation. It was way less depressing. "Sherry is pissed she is going to miss the big

38

meet. She begged her coach, her parents and the principal to reconsider letting the team go to state, but all three said no," she told him. Sherry's speech and debate team partied together and now all fifteen members would sit home and miss the most important meet of the year next to Nationals. Sherry had been preparing her piece for months. As a senior, it would be her last shot to win a spot at Nationals. "She feels so stupid they got caught," Mandy continued. "Sherry is on lockdown, and her parents aren't letting her go anywhere. Last night, she asked her dad to go study with Raine, and her Dad actually laughed at her and told her he would be happy to study with her." Derek and Mandy shared a laugh. "I love Sherry's dad's sense of humor. Of course, Sherry did not find it funny at all."

Sherry's boyfriend PJ had always been well liked by Sherry's father though, so he was always allowed in. Sherry began to share with Mandy about their make-out session, but Mandy stopped telling Derek more before the details were enough to make her blush. "Sherry thinks she and P.J. might be at the stage where he's going to say he loves her." Mandy smiled. She sure hoped some day she would have a boy tell her he loved her. Mandy always felt two steps behind her peers. While they were dating and planning what to wear to school, she was waiting for the next shipment of ice cream to come in the store, planning a new milkshake recipe to try, or playing with different sundae toppings.

"Sherry is under the impression she won't ever see me again. Of course that was the dramatic Sherry talking."

Sherry also told Mandy, Johnny and Wesley weren't debating together this weekend. Mandy had a hard time believing that. They were always the dynamic duo. She thought about asking Derek if he had heard anything. He was white knuckle gripping the steering wheel, and she thought it best not to bother him. Mandy knew P.J. thought he and his debate partner could have smoked the competition if Johnny and Wesley weren't debating together. For a minute, Sherry got Mandy's hopes up, because P.J. and Sherry talked about coming down for the meet. But Mandy was pretty sure if Sherry's dad wouldn't let her go to a friend's to study, he wasn't going to let her come down and stay in a hotel with her boyfriend.

Chapter 5

Gillian craned her neck. Louts and Stewart, toward the front of the Jackson bus, were animated as they practiced their drama piece for the Casper State meet. Several of the freshmen looked on in awe. Gillian, however, turned her attention out the window.

Participating in speech and debate in Wyoming was such a new experience. In Arizona, where Gillian used to live, the meets were one day. Generally kids only participated in one category and you never knew anyone else. But in Wyoming, every town had a team and the meets were weekend affairs that took hours to get to. And then each student often competed in multiple events and everyone knew everyone else.

Snow flurries were swept this way and that by the motion of the bus. Gillian wondered how the driver could even see the road ahead. *Maroon 5* played their latest hit through her headphones. She settled back, lifting her knees to rest against the seat in front of her.

Gillian never liked Yellowstone. Not even the first time when they'd visited, before her parents decided to take the job. Her mother and father believed it sounded like a great opportunity. A wonderful adventure. But Gillian had wanted to stay in Arizona with all her childhood friends. There her red hair didn't stand out so much, and she wasn't the only senior who stood five-ten.

How things had changed. This was exactly what she'd wanted ever since they'd moved to Wyoming. To leave. Get away. But it wasn't an option to return to Phoenix. Now they wanted somewhere safer.

When her parents had finally told her what was going on, it only confirmed her own suspicions. She'd actually sensed problems almost from the beginning. Before they'd moved to Jackson, her mother and father had insisted on dinner every evening as a family. This had always been an area of contention, with Gillian wanting to spread her wings and spend time with friends. Then, all of a sudden, it was her parents who urged her to get out. And when she was home, they'd eat a silent dinner together, and then excuse her to go to her room, where she'd hear their furious whisperings. Some of the nights, Gillian tried to fill the void in conversation only to be met with mute stares from her father and absentminded murmurs from her mother.

Gillian blinked several times coming back to the present.

Beyond the blinding whiteness, she searched for a landmark. Finding nothing, she reached in her backpack for her computer. She pressed the button and waited.

Since her parents had told her of the situation she had witnessed their furious labors. Her mother pulled up maps on the computer. She ran statistics, calculating this and that. Her father scoured books and analyzed data. No longer did her parents have to hide what was happening.

Gillian focused on her computer. She knew her parents would find a way. Of course they would. She never doubted

42

it. But when she finally heard their plan, she laughed and then sat stunned when they didn't join her.

"We have to," her father said. "It's a great opportunity. We are fortunate to have been asked."

"We must go," her mother said. "It's the only way."

And soon, Gillian was told, they'd be leaving soon. Ten days.

"What about everyone else?" she'd asked.

Her father shook his head.

"Grandmother? Grandfather?"

Her parents had not been able to meet her gaze.

Gillian looked at the twenty kids on the bus around her. She swallowed the lump in her throat. No one was to be told. No one. And what good would it do if she said something?

She startled when someone sat down beside her. Gillian pulled her earphones away.

"Can I go over some lines with you?" the girl asked.

Chapter 6

The Riverton team pulled into the parking lot of the Casper Holiday Inn at ten. Under the parking lot lights, snow glistened on the ground. Everyone hurried into the warmth of the building. A fire roared in the lobby fireplace. Coach Mark quickly handed out room keys and assignments. Four students per room. Cots were set up.

Johnny took his key and walked with Trisha toward her room. He loved how her dark brown hair flowed halfway down her back and shined in the light. At the door, he leaned towards her, his hair falling in front of his eyes. He swept it back the sexy way he'd practiced in the mirror. "I'll meet you in thirty minutes by the pool," he said.

Coach Mark, walking by at that moment said, "Johnny, curfew. Head to your room."

"Yes, Coach." Johnny looked at Trisha. "So, you wanna meet up?" he asked.

"I'm going to bed. Big day tomorrow," she told him.

"Okay. Well, if you change your mind, knock twice and run." He wiggled his eyebrows.

"Good night, Johnny," she said and giggled. Johnny lingered at the door and heard Wesley's whining nearby. Johnny chuckled as he listened to Derek and Wesley talk.

"Hey, man. You guys are getting in late, too," Derek said.

"We hit some snow and it slowed us down. What about you?"

"A slow bus driver. Rumor has it you and Johnny aren't debating together this weekend? You guys will make the Casper team's day, if it's true."

Wesley turned toward Trisha's door where Johnny still filled the frame with his body. Johnny nodded. Derek's eyes turned to him. "No way. Say it isn't so. Johnny gave you up for a skirt?"

"Yep! He's doing poetry. He's messing up my entire life for a girl, and now I have to do Lincoln-Douglas. No offense. I know that's your expertise."

"None taken, I look forward to the challenge of whopping your butt in some friendly LD competition. You want some help? We can go over some information before we head over to the school tomorrow."

"That would be cool," Wesley said.

"How about breakfast at six. We'll hit the main points your second biggest competitor might have."

"Second biggest?"

"Heck, yeah, baby. I'm your first and I'm not giving you my arguments."

Wesley grinned, said goodnight, and walked into his room. Derek stood fumbling with his key at a door across the hall.

Johnny slowly meandered toward his door. Observing the debaters around him. He had always been good at reading people. He would wait for someone to start talking and analyze the difference between their body language and the words coming out of their mouth. Derek and Mandy from Shoshoni were a perfect example. Derek was trying to act cool. Not let his sister know how much he loved her. Their conversation from a distance seemed casual.

"Derek?"

"Jeez, sis. Warn a man before you come up on him."

"So, it's true? Johnny dropped Wesley for a girl?" Mandy said.

Johnny wished he wasn't the only topic of conversation.

Derek nodded. "I'd kill him if I were Wesley." He shook his head. "That's why I do Lincoln Douglas."

"That, and who would be your partner?" she teased.

"Ha! Ha!,"

"Goodnight," she said. "See you in the morning."

"Night. Don't let the bedbugs bite." Mandy left her brother to walk to her room to join her weekend roommates.

This short conversation, instead of saying you bug me, get away sister, was filled with non-verbal information that told Johnny that Derek was very fond of his younger sister. He leaned in towards her when she spoke. Wrapped his arm around her in a half-hug when she walked away and listened intently when she spoke. No, he wanted her to believe something different, but it was clear to Johnny that Mandy was in fact Derek's best friend.

The hallways grew quiet and Johnny hurried towards his room. At home, on a weekend night he would've been up till dawn, out with friends or watching movies, but tonight everyone was asleep by eleven. Sleep deprivation was an enemy none of them could risk. For many of the players, it was their last chance at Nationals, and the last meet before they graduated from high school and moved on.

46

March 17th

Chapter 7

P.J. sped down the highway while Faith and Raine sang along with the radio. Behind them the sun peeked over the horizon. Sherry's father wouldn't let her come, but once the idea was out, P.J. decided he'd go to Casper anyway. They couldn't compete because they didn't have permission from their coach, but who cared?

"Gosh P.J.," Raine said. "You've got it so lucky."

"Yeah," Faith added. "I wish I could just go wherever, whenever I wanted. I had to beg big time."

"Me too," said Raine.

P.J., on his own since he was twelve, loved almost every minute of it. Now at seventeen, he was an emancipated minor. He stayed up late, ate pizza for breakfast, and never had to worry about somebody telling him he couldn't watch R-rated movies. He ate hot fudge sundaes when it suited him, and his parents stopped home every once in a while, back from some philanthropic trip, to say they missed him.

"So where are your parents now anyway?" Raine asked quietly.

P.J. shrugged. "I'm not sure. Last I knew they were on an island in the Pacific."

"Doing what?"

"Usually something the local government wishes they didn't do. That's why I have to wait for them to contact me. Most of the time they're in hiding.

They always brought him the most amazing gifts though and talked about elaborate castles and famous people they'd met. Then a few days later, they would rush out of town again to another destination. They saved wildlife, fed the needy, took medicine to underprivileged children. They saw human life at its worst, children starving, parents dying of AIDS and animals in the streets being killed for a little bit of fur, or meat.

"P.J.?" Raine interrupted his thoughts. "Bathroom break?"

Chapter 8

"You're up early," Mandy said and stared at the carpet. She had been on her way to her room when a door popped open and Wesley bumped into her in the hall, almost spilling her coffee.

"Sorry. I didn't see you," Wesley said.

He smelled good and didn't look too bad either. Mandy lifted her gaze and checked his attire - slacks, blue shirt and checkered tie - before she felt her cheeks become red.

"You're up early," she stammered again.

"Ah, yeah. Needed to get into the shower before the hustle and bustle begins. This meet can be crazy. But hey, I'm on my way to meet your brother. You seen him? We're going to run through some notes," he said.

"No, I'm not sure where he is in, but I'm sure he'll be on time."

"You want to join us?"

Mandy's heart skipped a beat, but she wasn't dressed and knew she'd better get going if she was to compete. "No, I have to get ready. I went to get some coffee." She lifted her cup.

"Oh, yeah, well you'd better hurry. It's almost time to leave," Wesley said.

"Thanks. I've got thirty minutes. Hey, good luck today," she added. Stupid, she thought. Why is it every time I open my mouth I sound stupid?

Mandy continued down the corridor, but stopped dead when she rounded the corner. Her jaw dropped. She'd never seen anything like this before at the smaller meets. Every hotel door appeared to be propped open. Girls ran room to room looking for approval of outfits. They borrowed makeup, hair ties and shoes. There were girls with their hair half done looking for gel or hairspray. A girl, who competed in extemporaneous speech from Shoshoni, limped down the hall with one shoe on.

"Anyone have a Band-Aid?" she yelled to no one in particular.

"What did you do?" Mandy asked.

"Ran into a door. Hey, you'd better hurry, or you're going to miss your opportunity in the bathroom," the girl advised.

Walking into her room, Mandy stopped short. There was no way she could get in the shower. Five girls from various teams and rooms were crammed into the little bathroom. One girl fixed another's hair, and behind a wall of hairspray, someone else worked on her make-up and ran through her humor piece, making sure each line sounded convincing.

Mandy slumped out and headed toward the bed. She was going to be the last one on the bus again, which would mean she'd have to listen to her brother's mouth.

"Honey, go in and use ours. I think Gillian went to breakfast so it should be empty," one of the girls said.

"Thank-you, thank-you. You're a lifesaver." Mandy grabbed her luggage, took the key from the girl, and promptly

52

headed towards the room. When Mandy opened the door to room 115 a redheaded girl sat on the bed staring out the window and chewing on a nail. Mandy immediately recognized Gillian.

Gillian glanced her way, but seemed to see right through her.

"Oh, my God. I'm so sorry. Your roommate said she thought you were at breakfast. She told me it'd be all right for me to take a shower, seeing as she's using my bathroom." Mandy kept rambling. Eventually Gillian shrugged and turned back toward the window. Mandy took this as a good sign and walked into the bathroom.

A quick fifteen minutes later, Mandy was showered, dressed, and ready to go. She re-packed her stuff and headed out of the bathroom.

Gillian hadn't moved from her perch.

"Well, okay. I'm going to leave." Mandy backed out of the room shutting the door behind her. She turned to see Gillian's roommate walking toward her down the hallway. "Hey, thanks for the use of your bathroom."

"No problem. You look nice." They passed each other. "Oh, I ran into your hot brother," the girl said turning. "He's looking for you."

"Thanks. Hey, is your roommate okay? She's sitting and staring out the window."

"Yeah, she's fine. That's how she is before a meet," the girl replied. "She's in her zone."

"Great. Okay, then, see ya," Mandy said.

"Good luck!"

Mandy returned her luggage to her room and then hurried to the breakfast area to find Derek. When she walked in Johnny stood with Trisha by the fruit at the buffet table. He twirled a strawberry between his fingers.

"Come on, baby, take my fruit," he said.

Mandy shook her head, and located her brother across the room. He sat with a disgusted-looking Wesley.

"I'm gonna kill him. I swear to God. He's a dead man," Wesley snarled as she sat down with them. Wesley's leg jumped beneath the table.

"Hey, sis." Derek gave her a nod.

"You guys done practicing?"

"Yeah. Ready to get on the bus? It's almost eight," Derek said.

Wesley still seemed focused on Johnny and Trisha across the room. "I can't believe him." He shook his head.

"Let me grab some toast first," Mandy said to Derek. She headed to the buffet. She liked the blond-haired and blue-eyed Wesley. He was nerdy, but cute. She wondered if he had a girlfriend. And if not, how she might get to know him better.

"Okay, if you don't want my fruit, how about a smile? That's all I need to make my day," Johnny told Trisha.

Trisha grinned. "Johnny, I'm going to go get my stuff and then head to the bus. You should do the same." Trisha walked away. Johnny's eyes were glued to her and he quickly followed.

Mandy shook her head. How could Johnny act that way? And more importantly, how could he hurt Wesley? She grabbed her toast and went outside with her brother to get on the bus.

As they crossed the parking lot she caught a glimpse of a girl with big black curls walking between two cars. She could have sworn it was Sherry. She stood on tiptoes, but then

54

Gillian stepped between them and blocked her view of the girl.

Mark, her coach, ushered her up and into the bus. He jumped on behind her and did a quick head count. He flashed a number at the bus driver and then went back into the hotel, she figured, to round up the remaining members of the team.

Mandy looked out the window. In the parking lot, it seemed other kids were standing around talking and waiting until the last minute to board their buses. She finished her toast and opened her window so she could listen to what was going on.

Right at that moment, Gillian and her roommate stopped beside the bus.

"Gillian, what's wrong with you?" her roommate asked. "Mandy said she came into our room and you were staring out the window."

"What? Nothing. It's an important meet, that's all. I'm trying to prepare myself," Gillian said. She brushed her hair back from her face.

Mandy's attention diverted when she heard Johnny scream across the lot. "Wesley, get over it. This is the girl of my dreams."

She saw heads turned and saw people from every bus quickly put their windows down to listen, too. Mandy shook her head. Johnny was once again stealing the show.

"This beautiful girl here in front of me is the only one I want. I'm going to marry her, after I win second at the poetry meet today – second to my gorgeous lady."

Wesley stepped up the stairs of the bus right next to hers and turned. He watched Johnny's antics for a moment. Mandy saw the Riverton coach quickly step in front of Wesley, blocking the door.

"Wesley, take a seat. It isn't worth it," the coach's voice boomed.

Whoops and hollers filled the air and Mandy turned her attention once more to Johnny. She was just in time to see him get down on one knee before Trisha. "Loving you, I can't see anyone else. You've captured my heart. Please take me. Fill my soul with your beauty and desire. Never let me go."

Trisha's cheeks turned cherry-apple red. "If you're planning on winning second, you should spend your time practicing because that poem isn't going to win anything." She turned her back and jumped on the bus. Johnny followed with puppy-dog eyes. Mandy smiled.

One by one, the buses pulled out of the hotel parking lot. Mandy felt the nervous energy that hung in the air. Everyone became quiet as her fellow students practiced lines in their heads.

The Shoshoni bus arrived at the school first. Mandy saw P.J. leaning against his car. She barely waited for the bus to come to a stop before she pushed her way through the crowd to the front. She leaped off and ran toward him.

"Where's Sherry? How did you guys get permission to be here? Aren't you going to be in trouble?" Breathlessly, Mandy fired off questions.

"Wow, hold up. One at a time. Sherry isn't here. Her dad said no. I came to visit, watch your brother debate, and confirm the rumor about Wesley and Johnny. Which I quickly got confirmation on from the show in the parking lot." Other seniors swarmed P.J..

56

Mandy walked off, sad Sherry wasn't there to support her. This was her first time at state and she was nervous. Entering the school, Mandy checked her watch. The school was filled. She'd heard Casper was one of the favorite schools to host competitions. Now she knew why. The school's recreation room was filled with pool tables and vending machines. Some kids played games while others listened to music or ran over their lines. Miss Sylvia, her coach, came up and handed her a schedule. Mandy didn't compete until ten o'clock, but Derek had a debate at eight-thirty. She decided to go and watch him.

Mandy entered the LD debate room and found P.J. in the third row. She joined him.

"Your brother looks a little pale," he said.

"He thinks if he doesn't win he won't get to leave Shoshoni. Then he'll be stuck running the ice cream shop forever."

"What?"

Mandy realized she'd rambled away her brother's dirty secret. Luckily the debate started and all conversation ceased.

An hour later, Derek walked out with win number one under his belt. He knew his topic inside and out. His competition never stood a chance.

Mandy headed toward her event, Student Congress. She wanted to make sure her notes were in order and she had enough copies of her bill. The room was quiet with only a few students, she didn't know, hanging around. She'd always loved the idea of someday working for the local government. And when she was younger, she'd use to wake up early and watch Federal debates on television. She'd spent hours researching bills being considered.

Mandy took her seat, pulled her notes out of their case, and piled them on the desk next to her.

Kids shuffled in and the session began. The first bill was to cap the senate's salary. Mandy listened to the first speaker, than someone re-rebuttled. Mandy walked nervously to the stage to refute the arguments.

"Americans are broke and America is broke. Yet, we continue to give money to congress." That was really all she had, yet Mandy rambled on aimlessly for two minutes. Finally, she wrapped up her speech, walked down the stairs holding onto the railing so she didn't fall. She sounded stupid even to herself and yet, she continued to stand and speak about bills. The session lasted forever. She would defend a position on a mock bill, stumble some, while never seeming to be able to make a clear and convincing argument. Each time she walked back to her seat more embarrassed than before.

The lights came up and Mandy gathered her things. Weakly, she smiled at the girl next to her. Tears threatened to spill over. She'd hoped to make a quick exit.

"It's okay," the girl said. "You did really well for your first time."

"Only it's not my first time." Mandy left, wanting to be far away. God, she was such an idiot. She stumbled into a poetry event, and slumped in the back row. Johnny was on stage performing a poem she'd heard he'd written.

> "Love, let's me whisper your name in the wind.
> Love, keeps me staring long after you've left my side.
> Love, holds me up when you smile at me. Love,
> charges through my veins moving me forward as you

sweep by. Love, cools my blood, after you heat it up.
Love, energizes my soul long into the night.
Your love is the cure to my teenage angst."

Suddenly, Mandy felt much better. No way was she that bad!

In the front row, Trisha sat rigid, facing forward. Johnny left the stage with a bow towards Trisha. Three more people did their pieces. Mandy left after the last person, not sticking around to see who won.

Eight hours later, Mandy was over her disappointment. She stepped on the bus exhausted, and slumped in her seat.

Derek, on the other hand, seemed to float onto the Shoshoni bus. She knew he figured a first place trophy was within his reach for sure. She'd heard he had mopped the floor with his competitors. The bus lit up with excited yells to support him. Seniors in the back broke into song. "We will, we will, rock you. Rock you." Derek stood proud flexing for the crowd, drawing them in with his easy smile and deep brown eyes until finally, their coach told him to sit down.

Mandy wished she could be that way. Instead she moved farther down in her seat, pushed her earbuds in and blared her music. If only she were on the Riverton bus. She heard Trisha had finally agreed to go on a date with Johnny after hearing his poetry piece. Mandy would have thought Trisha would have thrown up. But again, who was she to judge. Derek told Mandy before they got on the bus that Wesley didn't win today. She knew he would be disappointed and wished she were more confident. Maybe, he would confide in her and begin to see her as a friend. But as it stood, Mandy only said one or two word sentences before she stumbled. Derek felt bad winning against Wesley today, but he too had hopes of leaving his hometown.

Many students who didn't get scholarships would attend community college in Green River and she assumed this is what Wesley was now focused on. Of course this was not the start people like Wesley and Derek wanted. But Mandy was happy, she might get a chance to see Wesley on occasion when she and her mom went to Riverton to pick up something for the ice cream shop. She hoped he would quickly accept his loss and move onto new challenges. She didn't want to see him lose the spark that shown in his bright blue eyes when he talked. She had heard him whisper a quiet goodbye to the last debate of his high school career before getting on the bus, and it made her sad to think about.

From across the parking lot Mandy watched P.J., Faith and Raine piled into P.J.'s car. He looked up at Casper High School and saluted. He climbed in his car and then they were gone. Probably to get dinner somewhere.

Chapter 9

Johnny jumped on the Riverton bus. He didn't win, but didn't care. Trisha had finally caved and agreed to go on a date with him. He whistled his way to the back where he took his seat, Trisha at his side.

"Please can we stop and get dinner?" Johnny begged the bus driver. "I don't want some crappy hotel food for my first date. Come on. Help a kid out."

"I can't stop for just you, Johnny, no matter how much I like you."

"It's not just for me. Trisha wants to eat, too. I'm sure if we took a vote of who wants to go to the hotel and who wants Wendy's, Wendy's would have the vote."

"If you're so sure, ask everyone. If more than half the bus wants to stop and eat there I'll stop, but Coach also has to agree."

Coach shrugged. "Get your count," he said.

"Everyone listen up," Johnny turned and spoke loudly. "I want to take a vote and remember my fate rests in your hands. I can have a wonderful first date at a tasty fast-food restaurant or I can be stuck in a small back table with no lighting and a crappy waiter at the hotel."

Wesley rolled his eyes. "Stupid," he mumbled under his breath. Johnny ignored him.

"Come on, people. A show of hands for Wendy's."

Johnny walked down the aisle counting hands. He wasn't at all surprised to see Wesley's hand down. Jerk. He doesn't know what love is, thought Johnny. Johnny glared at him for not being supportive in something so important.

He and Wesley had been friends since third grade. They peed in the sandbox together. They built forts in the backyard and camped at the lake together. Wesley had been a friend and partner in crime for almost his entire life. They'd never been divided on an issue. Johnny couldn't believe Wesley wasn't there for him now. He'd never been so sure of someone as he was of Trisha. She was the one for him and this was his big chance to find love. He couldn't believe Wesley and how he acted like such a jerk, slumped in the chair, his leg bobbing and no expression on his face.

"Keep walking, Johnny."

"Why? What you going to do about it?"

"Johnny, you made your choice, and I've made mine."

"Well I don't care. I'm not living by your rules. I live by the 'Johnny rules' and they tell me we've been friends a long time. You don't need me. You're on your way out."

Wesley looked at Johnny in surprise. "That's what this is all about? You're pissed. I'm going off to college, so you're severing ties with me now?"

"You didn't listen to a word I said. God, you're acting like a girl. I'm trying to be nice here. You can make it on your own."

"Oh, well thank-you for clarifying that for me, because I was very unsure, probably because I sucked today."

"You don't know how lucky and smart you are. I can't leave the state and go to a bigwig college. I'm a small town boy with a ranch. I can never leave. I've always supported your dreams and I've never told you not to go after them. Trisha is my dream. She's hot with angelic skin, gorgeous eyes and she smells like cherries. So don't be a chump."

Johnny continued down the aisle counting hands. Thirteen were in favor. He wasn't going to get Wesley's vote, but it was okay because he had enough without it.

"Bus driver," Johnny yelled to the front. "I have your half and I'll raise you three." Johnny let out an excited war cry and then walked to his seat where Trisha smiled, waiting for him to take his place next to her.

Johnny gazed out the window, staring at snow and darkness. A small smile played on his lips as he remembered the previous summer when he and Wesley had gone to the lake fishing.

"Is your mom going to let you go to college in California?" Wesley had asked Johnny.

"No, she says the big city is too scary for someone like me," Johnny replied.

"She didn't. You're making that up."

"No, she did. Ask her yourself. She says it's okay for you to have big dreams and leave here, but well, Wesley boy, I'm country through and through. I have to stay. Anyway, who'd work the ranch?"

Johnny had known that moment would define their lives forever. Wesley wanted, no, needed to leave Wyoming, while Johnny would fight to stay. This fact hadn't impacted their relationship immediately, but both of them knew things would change. Johnny would have a ranch with cows, horses, ducks and sheep. He saw himself with a wife who'd love him, have his children and help take care of their land and livestock. He wanted seven kids and to ride rodeo. Wesley had listened to Johnny talk about how one day he would inherit the ranch.

But now, Wesley probably thought his friend was sacrificing him in an effort to reach his own goals. He didn't understand this was Johnny's chance at his dream. Johnny looked at Wesley. His friend sat quietly. Johnny saw Wesley smile but then it was gone. He turned back around. Johnny hoped Wesley would reach his goals.

When they climbed off the bus, the wind whipped and howled around them and snow flurries kicked at their legs. The team huddled close as they walked across the parking lot into Wendy's.

"Johnny, you owe us. We could be warm by a fire," someone behind him called.

The team rushed to the heat the restaurant provided. Johnny walked with an arm protectively around Trisha.

"You can order anything you want," Johnny told her.

She smiled, but didn't respond. They ordered and then found a quiet booth away from everyone. She stared at him. He looked away. It was as if she could see right through him. Sure, he could have afforded to take her to the restaurant at the hotel, but then he wouldn't know if she liked him for himself, or for his money and land.

"Can I ask you something?" she said.

"Sure."

"People are saying. . . um . . . Why did you choose me over Wesley?"

Johnny thought his breath had been ripped from his chest. "I didn't, Trisha. Listen Wesley has a big future at college, but I only had one chance to let you know I liked you."

64

"Why? I'm not going anywhere."

"I heard rumors." Johnny stopped and looked at her.

"Rumors?"

"This is dumb." Johnny's eyes pleaded with hers. "I heard the new kid, Paul, was going to ask you out. I knew I had to act fast."

Trisha started laughing, a deep chuckle that came from her belly. "Paul is my second cousin, you idiot. He isn't going to ask me out. He wants to date Victoria."

Johnny felt his cheeks burn. "Well, either way. Wesley doesn't need me. And I like you a lot."

"Hey, Johnny, your order's up," a teammate yelled across the room.

Johnny stood, walked over to the counter, picked up their food, and headed back to the table. He had to admit he was a little nervous. When he got to the booth, Trisha was gone. He looked around the restaurant, but didn't see her anywhere. He set the food down and then sat, feeling dejected. She couldn't even get through one meal with him. He looked up to see Trisha coming out of the bathroom.

He slapped his hand with his forehead. "Right, the bathroom," he whispered.

"What?"

"Nothing. Your fries are getting cold." He had to get a grip. It was nerve-wracking to be in love.

"Johnny," Trisha said.

"Yeah."

"Thanks for dinner."

Johnny stood, reached for her, and pulled her to him, one hand on her waist. He leaned down, gently brushing her lips with his. His desire built and he wanted more. He kissed her harder this time, parting her lips with his, to taste her.

"Lover boy, sit down and eat," Their coach called from across the room.

Johnny sat. He ate his fries with a huge grin. "I was right."

"About what?"

"You taste like cherries."

Chapter 10

Gillian shuffled to the back of the bus. She didn't remember competing, but must have because no one had said anything to the contrary. She didn't look around, but instead sat in the first empty seat and stared ahead. She reached into her bag to put on her headphones when she noticed her roommate frantically waving at her from outside. She lowered the window to hear what she yelled.

"You're on the wrong bus."

Gillian glanced up. Everyone looked at her. She felt color rise to her checks. Grabbing her stuff, she ran off the Green River bus. Lucky for her, students on the Jackson bus were distracted and didn't seem to notice. She shuffled to the back, pulled her hood over her head and turned her music up to block out the rest of the world.

At the hotel, she paced in front of the fireplace. It was growing ugly outside, but she wasn't worried about that. She couldn't reach her parents. Every night when she was away, they had an agreement she would call, a pact in place long before this other crazy stuff came up. It was their way of always checking in with each other, and now nothing. She couldn't believe they were unavailable. It wasn't like them, especially not since they'd told her what was happening. She quickly became worried.

Gillian hadn't wanted to go to Casper for a speech meet. Not now when she was beginning to meet people she could be friends with. Great. Once more, everything would be taken from her.

"You're going to break your phone if you keep dialing like that." A voice behind Gillian startled her. She spun around.

"Uhhh, Mandy right?" Gillian pulled for the name of the freshman.

"I'm going to grab some dinner. Want to come?"

Gillian didn't believe dinner would calm her, but she knew she had to eat. "Give me a minute. I need to try one more time to get in touch with my parents."

"Sure. I'm gonna run to my room. Be right back."

"Nothing," Gillian said a few minutes later when Mandy returned. "Let's go."

"You didn't get hold of your parents?"

"No. I'll call after dinner."

Mandy followed Gillian into the dining area, where they found a quiet place to eat. It was six, but the dining area was almost empty. People had either ordered room service or walked somewhere close to eat. Usually teams stuck together, but at State, it was all bets off.

"So, where are you from?" Gillian asked Mandy.

"Shoshoni. My parents own the ice cream shop."

"Oh. That's nice."

"You know. The one everyone stops at. That's how I know so many people. When I was a little girl, I'd sit and watch my parents serve tourists. I have to tell you, it smells so amazing when a shipment of ice cream comes in and you open the lids. The shop is small and quaint. A couple of years ago my parents re-painted it a really pretty green color with white trim. My mom told me I'd be good at running the store. When the shipments come in, I look over everything to make sure it's right. Then I go through and organize it all." Mandy looked up.

Suddenly Mandy seemed ill at ease. Gillian remembered those days herself when she felt she must sound dumb to someone else, someone older, or who had come from a bigger city. "Go on," Gillian encouraged her.

"I love the shop. I want to own it someday." Mandy looked at her hands. "But I'm not as good with words as my parents. My brother says I'll lose the shop if I don't learn how to talk. That's why I do speech."

"I don't think you're going to have a problem talking with people. You seem to be fine to me."

Mandy grinned. "You're easy to talk to. Do you get that a lot?"

Gillian smiled and remembered how at one time, she'd wanted simple things, too. "Are you and your brother close?" she asked changing the subject.

"Yeah, I guess. Do you have any brothers or sisters?"

Their waiter came to the table. They ordered food and drinks, and then resumed their conversation.

"I'm an only child," Gillian said.

"Don't you get lonely? I think I'd be if I didn't have my brother. When I was little, he was my only friend. Then one day he went off to a speech meet and left me all alone. That's why my parents suggested I join the team."

"You're lucky your brother is here. That must be nice."

Mandy shrugged. "Mostly I feel like a loser who needs her brother around to protect her." Tears began to form in the girl's eyes. "Sometimes it seems like I can't breathe when I'm in a room full of people."

Gillian nodded. "I've felt that way before too. Don't worry, it gets easier as you get older."

"I'm so glad I have you to talk to. You are so different now. When I saw you in your room this morning, you seemed distracted," Mandy said.

"Oh, I was just thinking."

"About the meet?"

"About when we lived in Arizona. I miss my home sometimes. My parents are scientists and we move a lot. But it's okay. They are really cool. When I was three we'd be in our basement for hours practicing drills."

"Drills? Ugh, like dance drills?"

Gillian laughed. "No, like natural disaster, catastrophe drills.

We would have gas masks, extra water, blankets, radios and even rationed food. My parents would make me stand in one spot for hours while they put different suits and masks on me, telling me the purpose of each one. It's funny when I think back on it."

"Isn't that child abuse? I can't imagine my parents putting a gas mask on me," Mandy said.

"Mandy, you never know when you'll have to prepare for something like that. And most of the time you only have a moment's notice."

They were interrupted by the waiter who served their food and left.

"I'm confused. Are your parents CIA? I mean who does stuff like that?"

Gillian shook her head and smiled. "No. Nothing that exciting, I assure you." Then quickly changed the subject as if the prior topic never occurred. "So what do you and your brother do in Shoshoni for fun?"

"We do a lot. We go mudding in his truck. We have cows, and we float down the river. Sometimes we walk the fields looking for cool leftover treasures from when Indians lived on our land. We play in the river on our tire swing; that sort of thing."

They ate dinner, talked about their lives, and shared happy memories. Soon Gillian had Mandy laughing.

When they finished, they headed toward their rooms.

"I still need to make a call," Gillian said.

"Oh yeah. I probably need to go find my brother. How about breakfast tomorrow?" Mandy asked.

"Um, sounds good. Seven?"

"Cool. See ya then."

Gillian waited until Mandy was clear across the room before she reached into her pocket, took out her phone, and dialed her parent's number.

"Hey, Mom," she said. Under her breath, she added, "finally." Gillian walked toward the lobby doors as she talked. "I just got done with dinner. I met this new girl. She's cool, small-townish, but cool. Her parent's own the ice cream shop in Shoshoni. You know. The one we always stop at. So, what were you and Dad up to?"

"Oh, we're busy preparing," her mother said.

"Preparing?"

"For the evacuation. You remember our conversation?"

"Yes, I remember. I, um, well I wasn't sure if that was what we were talking about here."

"Listen, I know you don't want to go, but we have to do this. It's what's in our best interest. What is the safest."

"I know, Mom. Love is in security," Gillian quietly said.

"I'll talk to you tomorrow."

She hung up and turned, running smack into Mandy.

"Oh, I'm sorry," Gillian said. She tilted her head and waited. Had she forgotten something? Left something?

"No, I'm the one who's sorry. I was just trying to find Derek. He didn't answer when I knocked on his door. I thought maybe he was outside."

"I don't see him. It's pretty quiet out there. Perhaps he's in the pool?" Gillian suggested. She started across the lobby with Mandy at her side.

"Hey, I wasn't eavesdropping or anything, but I heard you say something about love is in security. What does that mean?" Mandy looked at Gillian quizzically.

Gillian swallowed. "Um, you know," she stammered. Her phone rang. "Sorry," she said and answered.

Now Mandy would really wonder about her parents.

"We've been thinking. . ." she heard her mother say.

"Yes? Mom?" Gillian spoke into the phone. "Mom?" Mandy watched her. "Now what?" Gillian studied her phone and pushed a button.

The ground shook beneath their feet. Gillian counted the seconds before it stopped. She looked around. Nothing had fallen, and no one seemed to be anything but surprised that the power had failed.

She checked her cell phone and began to dial frantically. She walked down the hall toward her room, with Mandy following. Dialing. Dialing. "Nothing! The stupid thing has no bars. Great to have a cell phone when it won't work."

72

Mandy had tears pooling in her eyes. Gillian found a tissue in her pocket and handed it to her.

"I've never felt anything like that before," Mandy said. "What was that?"

A couple came out of the room across the hall, their children tucked protectively underneath their arms.

The guy searched their faces for answers. Emergency lights in the hallway flickered on.

"Sir, it was a mild earthquake," Gillian explained. The family wandered off in the direction of the lobby.

"An earthquake!" Mandy's eyes grew wide.

"It seems the phones are down." Gillian looked around. "And the lights are out. It's crazy. I wonder where everyone else is. How come no one has come out of their rooms?"

"My brother, Derek. I have to find Derek."

"I'll go with you." Gillian was surprised by the calm entering her body, even though she knew this was only the beginning of what was to come. All of the training with her parents had left her with the ability to move forward. She took hold of Mandy's arm and they hurried toward their rooms.

Mandy mumbled, "Derek hates living in Shoshoni. He can't wait to get out of town. But me, I want to stay there forever. We never have earthquakes in Shoshoni. Oh, my God. What if the quake hit there, too?"

"Easy," Gillian said. What she didn't need was to have Mandy panic. Everyone always did much better when they were able to maintain calm.

"The shop has been there for years. Everyone knows it. It's a staple in Shoshoni. No one can live without the ice cream shop. And my parents? Do you think they're okay?"

Gillian stared at Mandy. "It's best not to jump to conclusions. I'm sure they're fine. It was a mild quake," Gillian reiterated.

Mandy continued talking as if Gillian hadn't spoken at all. "I love ice cream. We have the best flavors. Nothing ever changes. You can always count on us for ice cream. It was just a little quake, right? No damage. I don't know what I'd do if anything happened to the shop. How would we live or survive? It's all my family has. All I have."

Before Gillian had time to take another breath, the lights started to come back on and her phone lit up.

Chapter 11

"So where to ladies?" P.J. asked.

The girls immediately started chattering. P.J. drove down the street looking for someplace to eat. The girls agreed on McDonalds and he swung into the parking lot.

They found a booth in the back by the play-zone.

"What a crazy day. Gosh, I wish Sherry was here," Raine said. "It would've been so awesome. She would've loved to watch Student Congress."

"Yeah. I can't believe her dad wouldn't let her come. He seems like such a nice guy sometimes, but then it's like he turns into a – a . . ."

"Sherry's dad is a great guy," P.J. spoke up. "She's lucky."

"Lucky? She didn't get to come to Casper. How can that be lucky?" Raine asked.

P.J. shook his head and finished chewing his Big Mac before answering. "She has someone around who loves her and cares where she is and what she's doing." He didn't say anything more for a second. He saw the dawning looks on the faces of the girls across the table from him. They suddenly were staring at their food as if searching for another topic.

"Everyone thinks I've got it made with my parents out of town. But really, it stinks."

"But you can do whatever you want," Faith said.

"Yeah, and I suffer the consequences of whatever I do, too. And it isn't easy. I get in trouble and there's no one to help me. I wish every day my parents would tire of being do-gooders and come home."

The girls ate quickly. P.J. finished his hamburger and sat drumming his fingers on the table. A minute later, Faith asked, "You ready to go?"

They left the restaurant and crossed the parking lot. His phone vibrated. He answered it quickly, but no one was there. Odd, he thought. Shrugging, he replaced it on his belt loop. They climbed into the car and headed toward the hotel where the other debaters were staying. P.J. tapped on the steering wheel as they drove.

"Why are you so edgy?" Faith asked.

"We should've been competing here. We could've stomped them," he said.

"We will next time."

P.J.'s mind wandered to their first meet together. Faith could have won without a partner. P.J. on the other hand, had been so nervous, he thought he was going to throw up. He ran a hand through his hair.

"Do you remember our freshman year?" Faith smiled. "Our first debate was a disaster."

"Why?" Raine asked.

"Well," P.J. started, "when we went on stage I was nervous. So Faith went first. I thought if she started, it would help calm my nerves a little and then I would get in the groove and rolling. Instead, when Faith went up there, she started using evidence to support the other side. She was talking and I tried to get her attention by waving my arms. I knocked water all over our evidence and when I jumped out of the way I kicked over the podium and the microphone. I did, however, finally get Faith's attention."

"It was embarrassing. I'm not sure why we ever tried debating again after that."

"Because, the judges told us you were so convincing debating the other team's position, they won because of you."

The trio chuckled.

They arrived at the hotel, and as they climbed out of the car, P.J's phone rang again. It was Sherry. But when he answered no one was there. "So, weird," he said.

P.J. walked into the hotel as the earthquake struck. He looked around in confusion. The concierge yelled something, but it was lost in a symphony of sounds. P.J. pulled Faith and Raine back out the doorway and away from the windows.

They heard the alarms of the cars in the parking lot outside.

P.J. thought it almost looked like a winter storm with flakes of ice showering down around them. He realized there was an alarm going off somewhere in the back of the hotel.

Chapter 12

Sebastian Navarro rode the fence. The day was warm and he smelled spring. His eyes shifted to the ground. So far he found two areas where new posts would be required before he could let the lambs and ewes out. His head swiveled to the east, toward home. He thought about the five hundred lambs currently living in the lambing bins with their mothers. He tipped back his hat and wiped away a thin bead of sweat that formed underneath.

Tomahawk, his quarter horse, picked that moment to stop. He lifted his head and quivered.

"What's the matter boy?" Sebastian searched the area for sign of a cougar, bear, or wolf. It was still too early for rattlesnakes.

Tomahawk whinnied and shook his head.

Sebastian saw nothing that would cause his horse to react so, but Tomahawk wasn't moving. Concerned for his favorite horse, Sebastian jumped to the ground with the reins still in one hand. The horse chose that moment to rise on hind legs and pull away. Sebastian was stunned. He tried to gain control, but his horse was crazy wild. Finally, Tomahawk yanked free and took off. Sebastian watched as he raced up over the hill and toward the ranch.

Sebastian briefly worried about his wife and children should Tomahawk enter the ranch-yard still out of control. Then he remembered they'd gone to Custer, after school, to shop. His family didn't plan on being home until after dinner.

He shifted his gaze to the fence and began the walk home. Sebastian figured he might as well finish checking the fence. Having taken no more than three steps, he noticed the fence posts far ahead waving in the wind. How odd, he thought.

A few minutes later, he arrived at the fence he'd seen moving and shook it, surprised to find it solid in the ground. More confused, Sebastian looked around. The air was calm. He couldn't even feel a breeze on his skin. His brow furrowed. What the heck?

The next thing he knew, he lay on his back, staring up at the sky. The ground beneath him shook and groaned. Tears formed at the corner of his eyes as he lay there praying. Never had he experienced such a thing. Agonizing minutes seemed to pass before the ground settled. Still Sebastian waited on his back to be sure. When he rose to his feet, he felt the bump on the back of his head and was grateful it wasn't bleeding.

His mind was in turmoil. He had no experience of earthquakes, but this one seemed bad. And he was frightened. A major earthquake in Newcastle, Wyoming? He remembered his father talking of an earthquake that occurred on the night he was born, August 17, 1959. A 7.1 earthquake centered in Montana and was felt in over half the state of Wyoming. His brothers always teased, he'd rocked the world when he was born.

Sebastian's gaze turned west, toward Yellowstone and he wondered if the National Park on the other side of the state was to blame. Turning back to the east, his thoughts returned home. He ran up the hill. At the top, he tried to make sense of what he saw. The ranch house and barn had collapsed and he saw no signs of life. Not even Tomahawk.

Behind where his house had stood, to the north, he saw a large ravine that hadn't been there that morning. Sebastian swallowed back his anguish and fright. He'd lost everything he'd owned.

* * *

Susan Navarro stepped into the Reader's Retreat Bookstore. "For just a few minutes," she told her two sons, who at eight and eleven, felt the need to groan. She'd often passed by the store in downtown Custer, and today, with Sebastian out riding the fence, it seemed like a good time to stop.

While her eyes adjusted to the dark interior, an elderly gentleman sitting at the counter asked, "Can I help you find something?"

"Oh, no. I'm just looking," she said. Intimidated, she scanned the stacks of towering books. "Wow!"

Dozens of ten-foot shelves rose to the ceiling, each filled with dusty used books.

"Your first time in here?" the gentleman asked.

When Susan nodded, he began the tour. He showed her how the books were organized and told her how most of them came from estate sales. "I have one of the largest collections of literature on Native Americans in the state. What do you enjoy reading?" he asked.

"Everything," Susan replied.

And so he kept taking her deeper into the store. The boys followed for a short time, but soon became bored with the whole affair and found some easy chairs at the front of the store to sprawl in.

"This is so boring," Eli said. "I thought we were going to buy new shoes."

Xavier shrugged. He picked up a large book that sat on the coffee table between them. He leafed through it, studying the photos from a century earlier. Soon, Eli was sitting on the arm of the chair with his head bent close.

When the earth began to move, Eli felt it first. Confused, he looked to his brother. Xavier shrugged and they turned the page. Minutes later, the moan and roar of the earth caused both their heads to snap to where they'd last seen their mother. The large shelf beside them tottered and weaved, unsure as to where it should go. Xavier grabbed his brother's collar and hauled him toward the door, while he attempted to yell to his mother over the noise. The windows of the store shattered behind them as the boys made it outside. Together they turned to watch for their mother, but were soon overcome by dust that rushed out after them. Thousands of used books fell to the floor. Only then did the two boys look around at the mayhem surrounding them on the street. They watched as, one by one, the buildings of Custer collapsed.

* * *

Twenty miles away, at Mount Rushmore, the earthquake's epicenter, the land rose and dropped without warning. It lifted the few late afternoon visitors off the ground and mercilessly dropped them onto hard rock. Those that

81

reacted quickly were able to rise and witness the crumbling of one of America's most revered monuments. When the earth finally stopped its frightful dance, the rocks that had been the delight of a nation were completely gone.

* * *

Honey and Jacob held hands and strolled along the riverfront. At eighty, they were confident their good health was in large part due to their daily walk. Married for almost sixty years, they had five children, and twice as many grandchildren and even a few great-grandchildren. The town had changed in the long years since they'd grown and raised their family, but not the river. That was a constant.

Jacob stopped and lifted his hand to point. "Look," he said and together they watched as dozens of birds took flight.

"Well, what do you suppose . . ."

Jacob turned his attention to the river, where fish flew up out of the water. "My God!"

Only then did they feel the ground beneath them move. Honey, fragile boned, fell hard to the ground, knowing in an instant she'd broken her hip. Pain enveloped her. She saw nothing of the water now heading right for her and her husband, as the river sloshed out of its banks.

Chapter 13

Johnny looked outside to see flurries softly coming to earth, covering the ground in a blanket of snow. It looked serene after the small earthquake. All was quiet except for a siren off in the distance. People didn't seem to be moving yet, not sure if the ground would stay still. A couple of kids laughed nervously.

Johnny saw two teammates hidden under a table. The lights in Wendy's flickered on.

"Now what?" Trisha asked.

"I think we're going to need…." Johnny began.

The ground shook under them with the fury of war. Walls wobbled and the entire building made an eerie noise. It was unlike anything Johnny had ever seen or heard. The windows buckled and he heard a sound like a suction cup popping. Johnny wondered if the earth would shake apart, open and swallow them whole.

Tables shifted, chairs screeched and trays slid to the floor. Two kids, who'd been under the table, were now trapped. The floor was littered with debris flung hap hazardously by the earthquake.

Johnny took Trisha's hand and started to run, Wesley was right behind them. They dodged ceiling tiles along the way. Rounding the corner, they headed down a small hallway.

Johnny heard a dull thud behind him. He didn't look back. Instead he pushed Trisha into the bathroom.

Trisha stared at him. Her eyes filled and tears spilled down her cheeks. "I'm scared. I don't think . . ."

"Wesley, shut the door," Johnny interrupted Trisha. There was no answer. Terrified, Johnny turned to see Wesley held hostage between a trashcan and the wall. He climbed over a table and the debris scattered between them. A loud boom came from a short distance away. The Wendy's windows gave and glass sprayed on top of them. Johnny ducked. He stood to see the cause of the shattering glass. A thick, black cloud of smoke billowed from what used to be a small gas station next door.

Movement in Johnny's peripheral caught his attention, and he looked to see Wesley. A large piece of the glass had sliced through the skin of his forehead. Blood instantly stained the front of his shirt. Johnny held his friend's glance willing him to stay focused and awake until the earth stopped shaking.

But Wesley's head slumped to his chest and his body went limp.

Finally Johnny reached Wesley. He took off his shirt and held it to Wesley's head. Wesley's eyelids fluttered but didn't open. Johnny's shirt was quickly soaked through, but he couldn't find anything else to grab. He continued to apply pressure, hoping soon he would be able to get his friend help, and all the while he pleaded with God. Inside, he felt his anger growing, causing him to shake. He couldn't believe what was happening.

As suddenly as the earth began vibrating, it stopped its terrible moaning and silence descended.

People in various states of shock wandered around the Wendy's. Most of the staff seemed to have quickly disappeared after the quake. Outside, snow continued to fall and stick to the earth. Johnny shivered and pushed one more time to get the trash can off his friend. He moved it enough to get Wesley out. Johnny felt Trisha helping him. He didn't know when she had come out of the bathroom, but feeling her warmth and love gave him strength.

They helped Wesley to lie flat on the floor. Again his eyes fluttered, but stayed closed. Johnny saw others moving toward the front door. Everywhere he looked, people ran to get out of the building. He wondered if it could collapse with them inside. He wanted to move quickly, but knew he couldn't move Wesley without help. Trisha was close by, but she'd stopped moving and instead stared at the scene in front of her.

"Trisha, Trisha." She turned in his direction, her mouth half open. "I need you to get Coach and a couple of other guys. We need to get Wesley out of here. Then I want you to stay on the bus and wait until it's ready to go."

Trisha moved slowly through the crowd until she found the coach, who knelt next to some students. She went over, spoke to him, and then moved about trying to help others.

"Get the injured students onto the bus. I'm going to take them to the hospital," Mark called to everyone.

"We need to help Wesley. He has a head wound," Johnny yelled in the confusion.

Johnny and Coach lifted Wesley. They carried him onto the bus and laid him on a cushioned seat, where his legs dangled over the end. Johnny returned to the restaurant and helped a few more kids get to the bus. He wrapped bleeding wounds with towels found from the back of the Wendy's, and checked on the injured as he left the bus to go back to help Coach.

Walking out with the last person, he boarded the bus. The driver shut the doors and headed to the hospital. Johnny crouched awkwardly in front of Wesley. He took over applying pressure to his head from Trisha. She sat on the seat behind him touching his back. They bounced along the road past what used to be the gas station. Police and fire trucks were there, trying to get the situation under control.

Johnny looked at Trisha. He mouthed, "I love you."

She said nothing. Her hazel eyes stared blankly at him. Her hands shook as she absently reached in her pocket and pulled out her lip balm. He hoped it was shock, but didn't know what to think of the silence. Maybe it was too much, too fast. He returned his gaze to Wesley. Wesley was a terrific friend. He would've never abandoned his debate partner to go after a girl. Johnny's shoulders drooped.

Trisha touched his shoulder. "I love you, too," she said.

Johnny tuned into the sounds on the bus. There was wailing and muffled cries of the injured. He found himself wishing the driver would go faster, even as he recognized they bumped along roads that had been damaged.

When the Riverton bus pulled up to the emergency entrance of the hospital, the place was in chaos. Johnny and some others carried Wesley inside. Others were taken in wheelchairs, walked or helped by nurses who came in waves from the building. The coach talked to someone at the front while everyone was off-loaded. Johnny went to find Wesley, but Coach grabbed his arm.

"Johnny, I need you to go back to the hotel with the uninjured. Tell the other coaches what happened. We'll need a plan. I'm going to be here for a while."

"I can't. I have to stay with Wesley."

"You can come back later. Right now, I need you to be with the team. Besides, there is no room at the hospital for any extras."

Johnny looked around. It almost appeared as if the entire town was crowded into the waiting area of the hospital emergency room. He bowed his head and reluctantly stepped on the bus. All of their wounded had been delivered. The coach waved the bus off and the driver got back on the road, heading in the direction of the hotel. Johnny didn't know why he had to go back to the hotel. He needed to tell Wesley how sorry he was. Let him know how much their friendship meant.

Johnny pulled Trisha closer and kissed her on the cheek.

Chapter 14

Gillian yelled into the phone, "Mom! Dad! We've had a tremor." Gillian walked away from Mandy to have privacy.

"We felt it here, too. It's okay, honey. Just a small quake. Remember to stay calm. Nothing major should happen for several days. It was a warning. Do you have power?"

"Yeah."

"Don't worry. Just remember your drills. We have time. We have tons to do; we'll call you later."

"Mom?"

"Yes, honey."

"I know it's going to get worse. I want you to know, I'm in. I'm ready to leave, too."

"Okay, honey. Bye."

Mandy joined Gillian. "What's going on? What's getting worse?"

Gillian took a deep breath. "Nothing. Look we have power." Gillian paused for a moment. "You need to stop walking up behind me."

Mandy stared at Gillian in disbelief. Gillian knew she'd heard too much.

They were still standing in the hotel lobby when the ground jumped beneath their feet and the earth started shaking again. Items around Gillian tumbled forward. In slow motion, she saw two bookshelves tip and lean together. Chairs pitched violently and people ran for cover. Gillian finally willed her feet to move. She found a doorway to stand in. "Dumb," she smacked her hand against her forehead. She had been trained for moments like this. She knew better. They had changed the rule. No doorways. Instead she needed to stand next to something strong, so if stuff fell, it wouldn't hit her. Her parents called it the triangle effect. Spying a filing cabinet, Gillian ran across the lobby, grabbing Mandy's arm and pulling her along.

Gillian couldn't believe the chaos around her. These people weren't ready for something like this, they didn't have major earthquakes in Wyoming. She watched the scene unfold in front of her. It was bad enough with one, but really, a second quake was unnecessary, she thought. At least she was in the right spot this time, with Mandy huddled next to her. Gillian could tell the freshman was trying to be brave, but she looked as if she were about to burst into tears. Gillian saw the main-floor hotel windows burst, and glistening pieces of glass showered the lobby.

Beside her, Mandy hovered closer to the filing cabinet. She squatted and covered her ears with her hands.

"I don't want to die," Mandy murmured.

Gillian didn't want to either.

"I want to go home. I want Derek."

Gillian wanted some things too, like for the ground to stop its motion. She prayed for her family, hoping that this wasn't the end already. She needed to be strong, take charge and help people feel okay once the shaking stopped. And it would stop. Her parents were never wrong; the timing was just a bit off.

She waited while the earth continued to rumble until finally the world stopped pitching and stood silent. Just like that, the earth was quiet, deadly still. All remained in their places, unsure if they should move. Seconds ticked by. Slowly everyone came out from where they'd hid.

Gillian assessed the damage in the lobby. Hotel staff ran about trying to calm guests. Someone yelled about backup generators that weren't working. Gillian wrapped her sweater around her body but shivered anyway. It was amazing how cold Wyoming became at night especially with no electricity. She figured if something didn't happen soon, she wouldn't have to worry about future happenings in the state. They'd freeze to death in a few short hours. They needed to find jackets and blankets quickly.

Miss Sylvia, the coach from the Shoshoni team, came running around the corner. "I need everyone to stay in the lobby. We need to gather all the students and head to the high school. This is bad. I think the school will be more stable. It was built with earthquakes in mind. I've already spoken to the Casper coach. They're going to meet us over there with supplies. My God!" She took a deep breath and then continued. "Mandy, find paper and pencil. Write down the names of everyone. We'll send other teams and coaches your way, too. Make sure you get home phone numbers and where they're from so we can start doing head counts. If they know of someone missing from their team, write that information also. What a mess! We've got some injured. I'll need to stay with them until they get help."

"Ma'am, perhaps we should check the rooms," Gillian suggested. "There might be kids who need help." She looked at Mandy.

Mandy smiled weakly. "That's a good idea," she said.

Miss Sylvia interrupted her. "Mandy, I need you and this girl to help get everything organized in order to leave. I'll need teams to search the hotel. I've got to focus on the injured. Can you handle this for me?"

While the coach spoke to Mandy, her gaze was directed at Gillian. She nodded in understanding.

Mandy and Gillian gathered the kids and adults who now were coming into the lobby. They organized people into groups to gather information and direct others to the Casper High School.

"I'm Gillian," She said and stuck her hand out to introduce herself to a gangly boy with unkempt blond hair who stood a bit apart.

"P.J."

"Can you come with me? I need to search upstairs for others. And we should stay together in case there's an aftershock. Hurry! Also we need to bring back any blankets or food we find. We're going to need supplies at the school."

"I want to come too," Mandy said.

Gillian saw Mandy's hands shaking. She could sense the terror the girl felt. But this was a chance to show her how brave she really was. "Sure," Gillian said.

As they went to leave, Johnny, Trisha and a ragged, scared group of kids came through the front entrance of the hotel, where one door still held on by a single hinge, with the other long gone.

"It's the Riverton team," P.J. said. He hurried over to them.

Gillian and Mandy followed.

"What happened? What can you tell us?" At least forty kids and adults crowded them in order to get details.

"Where are your coach and the rest of your team?" Coach Sylvia said as she quickly crossed the room to join them.

Tears streamed down Trisha's face.

Johnny held her, while he looked at the ground. "Coach is at the hospital with the rest of the team. He thought we'd be safer here," Johnny answered.

P.J. put a hand on Johnny's arm. "It's okay. I'm sure they'll be fine," he said.

Gillian tried to ignore the blood covering Johnny's clothes, but knew things had been serious.

"We were at Wendy's. The quake blew the windows out and a gas station across the street exploded."

Miss Sylvia walked away with a dazed expression on her face.

Gillian recognized the signs of fear taking control. She stepped closer to Johnny, Trisha and P.J.

"Okay," Gillian said, "can either of you go with Mandy? That way we can get through the hotel faster. We need to gather the rest of the teams here quickly."

"Sure." Johnny turned to Trisha. "You stay here." Trisha looked hurt at Johnny's words. "I'll be back soon," he said.

"I need to let my brother know I'm okay. I'll meet you upstairs," Mandy said.

"No. We stick together," Johnny told her.

P.J. and Gillian headed toward the stairs while Mandy and Johnny headed toward Derek's room.

"Derek!" Mandy saw him as he hurried down the hallway toward the lobby. She reached for his arm.

"Mom, Dad?"

Derek shook his head. "I don't know. My phone doesn't work." Mandy choked on a sob and her brother put an arm around her.

P.J. and Gillian watched from the steps.

"Thanks for bringing her to me," Derek said. "I'm going to take her back to my room."

"Your sister is supposed to go with me to find the rest of the teams and coaches," Johnny said.

"No way are you taking her. She stays with me."

"That's not the plan. We need to find everyone," Mandy said. She looked up at her brother. "I'll be fine.

I want to help."

"Okay, I guess." He hugged her. "Be careful," he said. "And Johnny, if anything happens to her..." his voice trailed off.

Gillian nodded to P.J. and they continued up the stairs. They stopped at the second-floor and listened for people. It was scary quiet. No panicked voices, no people shouting, no kids crying, nothing except the sound of car alarms still going off in the parking lot.

"Where's the staff and other guests? Why is it so quiet?" Gillian asked.

"I don't know. Let's start knocking on doors and see what we find," P.J. said.

"I just can't believe this," Gillian muttered. "My parents are always right. How could they not have known? How could they have been so wrong about the end?"

"What do you mean?" P.J. asked.

"Huh." Gillian flushed, realizing that her words had been spoken aloud. "P.J., it's nothing. Let it go."

"No, what did you mean? You said your parents were right? What's coming to an end?"

Johnny stormed toward them from the other end of the hall, Mandy behind, catching them both off guard. Gillian, took a step back startled.

"Gosh! You scared us," Gillian exclaimed. "It's too quiet on this floor. I don't think that's a good sign."

"You guys, we have to get moving," Mandy said.

Gillian stepped around P.J. and knocked on the next door. Mandy caught up to her and pounded on the opposite one.

"What's going on?" Mandy whispered. "We heard you talking."

Gillian turned to see Mandy nervously bouncing from foot to foot, waiting for an answer at the door.

"Leave it," Gillian said.

They finished their rounds of the rooms and then made their way back to the lobby. Mandy was talking about her hometown and something about her brother, however, Gillian had quit listening five minutes before. They stopped moving when P.J. saw Raine help Faith up from a chair in the lobby.

He rushed over. "What happened?" he asked.

"I tripped, fell into a suitcase and hurt my ankle."

"I'm pretty sure she broke it," Raine said.

"You want me to go with you to the hospital?" P.J. asked.

"No. Go to the school. Get home if you can. When the power is back on, I'll call my parents and have them come get me."

Faith hobbled toward the bus with help from Raine.

Miss Sylvia gathered the students. She laid out the plan for those who had joined the crowd. "You'll head over to the high school. Stick together. I don't know if they have power, but you should be more comfortable there. The Casper coach seems to think it's the safest place in the city."

She turned to the two bus drivers who waited for directions. "We found fourteen wounded. One bus will take them to the hospital and drop them off to Mark, the Riverton coach. Make sure he knows the names of everyone and where they're from, so parents will know where to find them."

Johnny stepped out of the crowd. "I'm going to the hospital."

"You can't. I need you to help."

"P.J.," Derek hissed. "You going home?"

"Don't know. Why?"

"We need a ride. I need to get my sister to Shoshoni. I'll make it worth your while."

Mandy grabbed a load of blankets and her suitcase. "P.J., please, we have to get home. I need to make sure my parents are okay," she begged. They trailed P.J. to his car. Gillian followed helping to carry Mandy's blankets.

"I can't. There's just no . . ." P.J. stopped short. "Dang!" he said. Then he turned on his heel and walked back inside the hotel. He returned seconds later with a handful of pillows and blankets and climbed onto the bus.

Gillian and Mandy stood in shock. P.J.'s car was tipped on its side between two cars. The wheels and the back window had been demolished. With no other option, they boarded the bus behind P.J. Guess Mandy wouldn't be going home anytime soon either. As Gillian sat down next to Mandy she saw for the first time the scared looks on her teammate's faces and the glazed terror in Mandy's gaze.

Chapter 15

Jessica Renfro stepped into the deli and stood at the counter considering what looked good for dinner. In front of her, an elderly woman waited while her pastrami was sliced. The neighborhood deli was her go-to-place when life got her down. Work was going okay, although she was frustrated it was taking her so long to get her face in front of the camera for any length of time. She was tired of doing the strange feature stories. But her real issue was Pete. What a jerk! She couldn't believe a man had fooled her again.

The ring of her cell phone caused the elderly woman to give her an annoying look.

Jessica turned away and answered. "Hello," she lowered her voice.

"Where are you? We need you to get to the station right away."

She stepped outside and onto the sidewalk. "What's going on?" she asked.

"We have an initial report of an earthquake centered in South Dakota."

"And you want me to cover the story?" she asked thinking about what she would need to take with her to the airport.

"No! We need you here at the station. Michael Davis is already there. He was visiting family. We need you to handle the news desk."

Jessica's fist pumped the air as she resisted the urge to scream, "yes!" into the phone.

"Are you there? Jessica? Don't tell me we've lost . . ."

"I'm here. No, everything is fine. I'm two minutes away. I'll be right there." She hung up the phone and looked up and down the sidewalk. Alone, she smiled, clapped her hands and then jumped into the air. It was a great day.

* * *

"This is your Six o'clock World News Tonight with Jessica Renfro."

Jessica was thrilled and frightened. This was her first big opportunity after months of waiting in the wings. Most of the world was still in shock. Not more than minutes after receiving the initial reports from South Dakota, the former Soviet Union informed the White House they, too, had experienced an earthquake of monumental proportions. The Russians were still trying to tally the fatalities, but the number was expected to be well over two thousand. The world was in panic again as Tsunamis struck Indonesia and New Zealand. It seemed an angry earth was coming apart.

"Thank you and good evening." Jessica pursed her lips and focused on the teleprompter. "Tonight we start with our top story. This evening at approximately 6:47 Mountain Standard Time, an 8.6 earthquake shook the ground of Northwestern South Dakota. Centered at Mount Rushmore, the quake was felt as far away as Idaho Falls, Idaho."

Moments before the show, contact had been made with someone from their South Dakota affiliate, but now a standard headshot was thrown up on the screen. She heard in her ear how contact was lost. She read the words from the teleprompter, "It seems we've lost all contact with South Dakota. What little we know at this time is . . ."

"The signal is lost," she heard someone in her ear.

I know, she thought. So tell me what to say, but the teleprompter was silent. She looked to the cameramen surrounding her. Finally, one stepped back. "Something is wrong with the satellites. We're dark," he said.

Jessica couldn't believe her luck. Her fist hit the desk hard.

* * *

Sebastian Navarro stood stunned in front of what was left of the ranch. The barn had been completely flattened with the shock. Now he examined his home. Its back was broken with the northern half splintered and warped, but the southern part of the house, though tilted, stood. He shook his head grateful his family was safe and in town. He couldn't imagine what had happened to his land.

He heard a noise and turned to see Tomahawk gallop over. "Good boy," Sebastian called. He walked calmly toward his horse and took the reins while he checked Tomahawk over. "You're lucky you didn't end up in the new ditch." Sebastian rested his head against his horse and felt him tremble. A cold wind blew and caused him to reflect. He didn't dare go inside the house. No, an aftershock could easily pull the rest of the frame down on him. Instead, Sebastian sat outside facing the road, watching for the lights of his wife's car. He could have ridden to the nearest ranch a few miles away, but didn't want his wife to worry when she came home and found him missing and their life destroyed.

The sun began to find its way behind the mountain and Sebastian decided to start a fire. He pulled wood from the barn and the north side of the house and used paper he found to start a bonfire that lit the entire yard. When darkness firmly descended, Sebastian grew concerned. It was not like his wife to be this late on a school night. With no moon shining, he sat and waited, warmed by the fire, wondering if whatever had happened was greater than he'd believed.

His eyes scanned the landscape around him, but saw no signs of other fires burning. Finally, reluctantly, he allowed his eyes to rest.

Chapter 16

"Mr. President!" The National Security Advisor waved a brief in the air as he rushed into the conference room located deep in the bowels of the White House. The luxurious interior was furnished with plush leather chairs and a table, fit for fifty, was filled to capacity.

"Please, tell me you have something," The President said.

"Sorry, sir, at this time we've been unable to confirm if the vice-president and his family made it to NORAD."

"You should be getting ready to leave," the chief of staff, Marvin Hardy, said.

The President turned to him. "Have we established the cause of the nationwide power outage?"

"We've only been able to gather small bits of data from a few local sources."

"Just tell me, can you verify if this was a terrorist attack?"

"We're still gathering information. I can't give you a definitive answer. We've been unable to contact our underground agents in foreign countries."

"What about domestic threats?" He turned to the head of the CIA, Will Gilbert. "Please, tell me you haven't been keeping anything from me?"

"Sir, no single group we've been watching has that kind of capability or technology."

The chief of agriculture, Sean Weston, leaned across the table and demanded, "What about the ESP?"

Beads of sweat formed across Gilbert's brow. His mouth churned, but he seemed to be having a difficult time forming the words.

"Spit it out," The President demanded.

"Mr. President, there is a device we have that could do something like this. However, we're still in the testing phase." He pulled his handkerchief from his breast pocket and wiped his brow before turning to Weston.

A smile spread across Weston's face. "National Enquirer tells all," he quipped.

"Do we know if the Yellowstone issue is in anyway related to the power outage?" The President asked the room. "Where is the science professor that was supposed to be en route here an hour ago?"

An aide from behind the crowd stepped forward and spoke in a whisper, "Mr. President, we don't know."

The President sighed, trying to regroup. A moment later, his secretary entered the conference room with a pudgy man behind her.

"Who are you?" The President demanded.

"Sir. I'm Milton De'vo. Professor Milton De'vo," the man stammered.

"Well, give me something. Has the Yellowstone caldera erupted?"

Milton De'vo's eyebrows rose as his eyes grew wide. "Uh, Mr. President, I don't know."

102

Chapter 17

It was too soon. Way too soon. Gillian's mom, Bridget Turner, felt her way to the kitchen, opened a drawer and took out the lighter and emergency candles she kept handy. She made her way around the living room and lit all of the decorative candles that had never been used before. Bridget found several more that were only brought out during the holidays and placed them about as well. Finally, feeling as if there was enough light, she went over to look at the information and charts that covered what had once been their living room wall. In the den, she heard her husband trying again and again to use the telephone. Soon, he too would realize they were cut off.

Bridget stood in front of the graph showing the ground swelling of Yellowstone's volcano. It had been monitored twice a day, and there were no significant changes that would signal the time for evacuation. Yet, a major earthquake had moved the earth to the east. Bridget fought to make sense of the situation.

The earthquake had to be connected.

"The phone lines are down," Cal told his wife. "And the radio isn't working. I tried new batteries."

Bridget forced a smile. "So, what do you think?"

Cal's gaze turned to the wall now as well. "I think we missed something," he said.

Bridget nodded. "Do you think it's too late?"

Cal didn't answer. He rubbed his forehead, as if trying to knead the knowledge out. "No, it's probably an early shaker. It can't be connected. The wildlife is still in the park, at least they were this morning when Mike went on his rounds. The rest would have fled if this were related to Yellowstone."

"Couldn't they be fooled, like us?"

He shook his head. "This is nothing to worry about."

"So we shouldn't head to Dulce?" she asked.

Cal walked to the window, pulled back the drapes and looked outside at the falling snow.

Bridget, normally so calm, felt tears slide down her cheeks.

"Pack lightly. One bag for each of us," her husband announced, his face grim.

"Gillian?" Bridget's hand moved to her mouth to hold back a sob.

Cal was instantly beside her. "We're going to go get her," he assured, his hands on her shoulders. "Now go. Hurry."

She knew he could feel her body shaking. As she turned, she saw her husband grab his parka. "What are you going to do?"

"I'm not sure we can use the car. We could try the roads to Casper, but that was a strong quake and right now, we've no information on damage. I think it'd be better if I go find Nash. He can fly us out."

"Not in this kind of storm he can't!"

104

"This spring storm is supposed to blow over by morning. Most of the other evacuees are already at Dulce waiting. We should join them as soon as possible, in case they decide, based on this event, to leave earlier than scheduled. Nash can get us there in hours, even if we wait till the storm moves through. And we can pick up Gillian on the way."

"What will you tell him?"

"That we have an important meeting regarding the earthquake we must attend, and need to pick up Gillian on the way. Nothing more."

More tears fell. She hurried away, eager to get busy with something that would occupy her thoughts.

An hour later, Cal stomped in and found her sitting in her jacket on the couch. Several blankets were tucked around her legs. Three bags sat lined at her feet. Cal smiled. Littered around the bags were additional items he knew she'd pulled out when other things of importance wouldn't fit.

"Well?"

"Nash says the telephone lines are down and so are the satellites," Cal said.

"Uh huh."

"He also said the storm was already easing, and getting out at first light shouldn't be a problem. We're supposed to head to the airport and meet him at five."

Bridget looked at her watch. The candles were so difficult to get used to. She blinked twice before she was able to focus her red-rimmed eyes. Ten-thirty. "I tried the radio again. Used batteries I knew should've worked. Nothing."

"Yeah, I ran into a few people out and about. They said the same thing. Kinda spooky."

"So now what?" Bridget asked.

"You should try to sleep. We could have some very long days ahead of us. The Aurora is probably not quite ready for flight. We might find ourselves hurrying to get it off the ground."

Bridget's hand came out from under the blankets. She held her cell phone to him. "I forgot to turn it off. I kept trying to get Gillian." Bridget swallowed back a sob. "It's dead," she whispered.

Cal reached into his parka pocket, pulled out his phone and quickly turned it off. His shoulders hunched, he went to sit beside his wife, burrowing under the blankets with her.

"It's so cold," she said.

"The hospital has an emergency generator and so does the school. People are congregating there to stay warm," he told her. "We could, too."

"I couldn't," she said.

He knew that would be her answer. For days now, it had been difficult for her to be around anyone but him. The knowledge of what was going to happen to the planet was eating at her.

"Then, let's get cozy," he said and wrapped his arms around her.

"We should've rented a place with a gas stove," she said.

He smiled. Bridget was always practical, even after the fact. "What's with the teddy bear?" he asked. It was perched on the table beside her. Cal recognized it as Gillian's first bear, one ear having been ripped and mended.

"I thought she might like to have it, but I couldn't fit it in."

"Close your eyes," he said and pulled her head close.

106

Cal was grateful when he heard her breathing slow and felt her drift off. He wished he could've followed his own advice, but the memory of the charts, graphs and information they'd gathered swam in his head. He couldn't make sense of it all. They should've had months yet before anything like this happened. His gaze turned to the window, where his wife had pulled back the curtains so they could see outside. He thought how having them open cooled the room even further, but he, like his wife, preferred being able to see outside. Darkness had firmly settled and he couldn't see any snow falling from where he sat, but he knew the cloud ceiling was still low. He blinked and went back to thinking about how they must have missed something. The quake was too close, and the damage apparently severe, as they had no phones or power. He prayed Gillian was safe.

Chapter 18

Soluma-Rah stood at the console and waited for the other Beings to appear. Her advisors remained out of sight and appeared ready for whatever would come. She could only hope with so many united, Ka would know he could not win this fight.

The host of heavenly bodies waited for the last to arrive, Bodha and his Beings were not as advanced in space travel and so had taken longer to join their forces, but now all of the Federation of Life Sources were present. Behind Soluma, scenes were being transmitted from the Water Planet. Chaos. Total chaos.

∞-As many of you know, earthquakes have shaken the Water Planet. Beings have perished. In some places, a great number.-∞

Although Bodha had been the last to join, he'd already heard and now was quick to think. His people would not tolerate lies. For their sake, he must advance peace above all else. ∞-It was too soon for the Water Planet to experience such trembling.-∞ his thought transfer was heard.

∞-The Water Planet trembling did not come from the land itself. It was caused by . . .-∞ Ora-J thought.

∞-I advanced our plan,- ∞ Ka loomed larger in his console. ∞-There is no way the Water Planet beings would leave if they did not know what their fate would be. This was a most important action and I am proud to have helped start things. I impacted them in mostly unpopulated areas, and the loss of life was insignificant due to the fact I concentrated the beams. We cannot sit and wait for them to feel fear and wish to leave. Bodha and others would never transport unwilling beings. So . . . now, I am sure, they will be ready to go with us. I would expect your pleasure from my most astute action -∞

Bodha and Soluma-Rah were both shocked by Ka's admission. They surveyed the rest of the council and read their thoughts mirrored in the other Beings.

∞-The council should have met and approved such an action.-∞ Bodha's thoughts were furious.

∞-What do you know of these beings?-∞ Ka demanded. ∞-We have studied them in the past. We know them.-∞

Some the council knew this to be untrue. They believed Ka's Beings had continued to study the Water Planet beings, taking them and removing them from their beds even recently. Soluma thought Ka's Beings went often to the planet and, while she wondered what they had done to the entities, she did not bring the matter before the council. Yes, she was Most High Elected, but Ka was lord of an angry planet. One who, before The Great Agreement, was filled with war. Soluma decided to pick her battles with Ka. Now, she wondered how Ka would take her decision.

∞-Ka, you have acted without common thought.-∞

The other Beings appeared startled by Soluma's pronouncement.

∞-I know, Most High Elected, Ka acted without common thought, but what was done will benefit our common goal.-∞ Rohongra had been quiet, her thoughts closed. Personally she did not agree with what was happening here or on her planet, but what could she do? They must have the Water Planet beings.

∞-I believe we should continue with the evacuation. It should be done much quicker now and we can all return to our planets.-∞

Numerous Beings fought for thought. Soluma calmed them all. ∞-Rohongra, I feel your thoughts, but this is a serious matter. We do not know how long it will take to evacuate some of the Water Planet beings. We could be here for many rotations. We must be in agreement and we must be able to trust. Ka's actions show him to be one who cannot be trusted.-∞

Ka's being rose and he shook. ∞-How do you dare say that?-∞

Soluma cut Ka's tirade off immediately. ∞-I dare by the position of Most High.-∞

Silence reigned. Bodha's breath was painful. He hoped his friend had not been correct. Would they all now find themselves at war with Ka? He searched his ship for his first companion. Momur stood at the ready. Of all the planets, not only were their ships the least prepared for travel, they were also the least prepared for battle.

Bodha knew his friend was ready to do what was needed to protect those on their ships. He waited for Soluma's next thoughts.

∞-Ka, I ask you return to your planet, now.-∞ Soluma-Rah declared. ∞-You shall collect no beings.-∞

Rohongra cut off Ka's war cry. ∞-Ka, the Most High Elected has spoken.-∞

110

Ka directed his hatred to Rohongra and then, realizing they were in close alliance, he cut off his thoughts and gathered his being. When his thoughts were open again, he nodded. ∞-I will abide by the Most High Council. We shall depart immediately.-∞

Ka's host left the meeting. The others waited until they felt his Being move away before they sighed.

∞-It is now up to us to come up with a plan to contact the beings below and help them. Bodha, as a Most High Elected and a messenger of peace, I shall await your thoughts.-∞

Bodha acknowledged the honor and left the meeting.

* * *

∞-We will gather more Water Planet beings. Send a messenger to Ka to let him know. He can be assured I will collect as many as possible,-∞ Dahi thought.

Rohongra understood. What a mess. Dahi had come along to supervise the transfer of disposables, as he called the evacuation of Water Planet beings. He had stood behind her and forced her to support Ka.

∞-How are we to gather more beings?-∞ thought Rohongra.

∞-I've already begun to make adjustments to our transport discs. We will have more room for beings. We are still in alliance with Ka. We must continue to support him. He has been disgraced. If he doesn't know we support him, his vengeance will be strong. Already we should prepare for the retribution he will reap against Soluma-Rah. But be assured I've got it figured out. Ka was right, he as made the task so much easier for us. The Water Planet beings will be eager to come now.-∞

* * *

Omis entered Ka's presence. ∞-We are ready to leave,-∞ she told him.

Ka's ship had left the Water Planet's orbit, but not before receiving a message from Dahi. Yet, he still had not given instructions to set the path for their return home. Omis came and rested her head against his, aligning their thoughts.

∞-You were right in what you did. The beings would never leave their planet and would have fought. We know that, but the other Most High Beings have no knowledge of the Water Planet's strength. They shall learn and then they will come back to you and ask for your advice. Be patient, my precious.-∞

Ka became one with Omis' thoughts.

Still he raged. They could not be at the mercy of ThAak-toons. Even though Dahi seemed to support him, he could never be sure of them. Rohongra made him nervous.

∞-Perhaps we should wait nearby,-∞ Ka thought.

∞-The red planet would abide us,-∞ Omis concurred.

∞-We've left much there from previous raids. We can move our ships deep within the craters and wait.-∞

∞-What of Soluma-Rah?-∞ his precious questioned.

∞-Who?- ∞ Ka asked and chuckled.

Chapter 19

Gillian, Mandy, Johnny, and P.J. continued to walk the hallways. They knocked, waited, counted and knocked again. The entire hotel staff seemed to have deserted the place.

Upon entering the hotel lobby, Gillian learned her coach had been seriously injured and was on her way to the hospital. She then heard the Green River and Laramie teams were lucky enough to find all their teammates and had left for home.

Riverton's coach was still at the hospital, leaving Miss Sylvia, the Shoshoni coach, to manage everything. She would rush through the lobby, ask for a head count, and then frantically head in the other direction.

Gillian was sure they'd been through the entire hotel, but she didn't want to be idle.

Finally, after the fifth time they'd gone upstairs, Miss Sylvia decided it would be wise to start busing students to the high school. Power still hadn't been restored and the temperature was dropping.

Once at the school, the bus driver gave them strict instructions to keep everyone inside. He left to pick up the remaining students still at the hotel. Gillian worked with P.J., Johnny, and Mandy to get people organized.

"Hey, I need names of everyone and the supplies you've brought," said a coach, who Gillian thought was from Casper. "Who's wounded and who's still missing. I need to know where we are with stuff."

He continued to shoot questions before any of them had a chance to answer.

Gillian opened her mouth.

"Never mind, I'll read your notes," he finally said, taking the list out of Mandy's hand and moving off.

Gillian stared after him. "Jerk," she whispered. "What should we do now?"

"Stay out of trouble," he said, apparently hearing her. He walked away, his head down straining to read the paper.

"I'm not waiting around here," Gillian said to no one in particular.

"The school's pretty big. We should stay together," Mandy argued.

"Fine, come with me."

"Please, Johnny, let's stay here," Trisha whined.

"I'd feel better walking around. You get a spot for us. We'll be back soon. Stay close to Derek."

Johnny brushed her lips with his.

They wandered deep into the dark school looking for unlocked classrooms and food. They had one flashlight between them, which was barely enough to let them see in front of their faces.

"I wonder how long we're going to be stuck here?" Johnny asked.

"Me too," Mandy whispered. "I want to go home." Tears started to stream down her face.

114

"It's okay. You'll get to go home." P.J. wrapped an arm around her.

"Maybe," Gillian said.

"What does that mean?" P.J. inquired.

"Nothing." Gillian turned a doorknob and they entered a large classroom with posters of space decorating the walls.

"Wow, this room is cool." P.J.'s face lifted to see the glow-in-the-dark constellations placed on the ceiling.

Gillian stood at a window. At first she wondered if it was snow coming down or ash. Then she remembered how her father had said the volcano would create a sonic boom and explosion that would take out all of Wyoming.

Gillian's thoughts moved to her parents. She was sure they'd have no choice but to leave her behind; that is if they were still alive. She wondered where the quake had been centered. And how soon the end would come. She knew originally her parents had thought they'd have at least ten days or so. Time was definitely ticking down. Tears filled her eyes. What should she do? What if they were gone? She held back a sob. She should've taken her parents' plan seriously. Mars was the only safe place they could evacuate to. All other locations were secondary.

"Gillian, Gillian." Mandy called from across the room to get her attention.

"What? I don't know anything. Can't you leave me be?" Gillian turned and yelled.

Everyone stopped and stared at her.

"I wanted to know if you were okay," Mandy's voice became smaller.

"I'm fine." Gillian said wanting to return her gaze outside.

"You think there are other life forms out there?" Johnny asked, pointing to science posters on the wall.

"Of course. The universe is way too big for us to be alone," Gillian stated.

"I want to go to the moon. I think it'd be cool to be an astronaut," P.J. said.

"What about if you had to live there for the rest of your life? Would that be cool too?" Gillian stopped. She hadn't meant to be so open.

"What do you mean by that? Seriously," Mandy asked. "What's going on? You've been making strange comments all day. Are you going to the moon? Does it have something to do with your parents?"

The boys stood still, watching her. Gillian took a deep breath and let it out slowly. Why not tell? What difference did it make? "I wasn't supposed to talk to anyone about it. But I guess it doesn't matter now.

My parents are scientists who work for Yellowstone Park. We moved here because there were problems. The Yellowstone Volcano is getting ready to blow. And that earthquake, well it was probably a warning."

"What? Oh my God! So is the government going to evacuate us?" Mandy asked.

Gillian shook her head. "The planet is no longer safe. The world is going to be ripped apart. We were supposed to leave to start a new colony on Mars."

"How come I . . . we haven't heard about this?" Johnny quipped.

"Yeah, what about that?" P.J.'s voice rose.

"There are only so many seats on the Aurora," Gillian explained. "But you might get into one of the underground

116

bunkers. If you're lucky enough to win the lottery, that is. Everyone else will have to find their own shelter from the ash and magma. God! If only we had a way to get to Alaska or Arizona," Gillian said.

"Arizona?" P.J. asked.

"Arizona's outside the red zone. And they have a bio-dome."

"A what?" Mandy asked.

"A bio-dome. At one time it housed scientists doing an experiment on whether we could live in harmony with biomes and create our own survival within a small space. It's meant to be used as a habitat on the moon or Mars. In the event of an emergency, like the Yellowstone eruption, it could be sealed shut. We'd be fine if we could get there."

"I thought I learned in science the Bio-dome had issues back in the '80's," Johnny said.

"They've fixed all the problems. You see, the government knew this mission to Mars was going to have to happen more than two years ago. It was the human race's only hope. Scientists have been working around the clock to make sure the idea of an enclosed space would work."

"You're a fruitcake!" P.J. turned his back to her and laughed.

"I'm still stuck on Mars. You're going to live on Mars while the rest of us die?" Johnny asked.

Mandy searched the floor. "I need to get home," she said. Her eyes filled with tears.

"Listen, my parents went to a conference at the bio-dome a long time ago. They have dorms, a kitchen, and the ability to grow food. We could be safe there. But we're running out of time. We only had ten days before we were to leave for Mars."

"What about Alaska? Is that a better place to go?" Mandy asked.

"Alaska is outside the initial blast zone, too. Either would be far enough away to be safer, but, I need to tell you, no one will be unaffected. In three days the ash cloud will reach the east coast. A week later and the ash will be in the atmosphere of the planet. Once that happens, all plants will die. It will only be a matter of time before animals are killed, too. It will be a nuclear winter that will last two years at least."

P.J. shook his head, "I still think you've lost your mind. I'm outta here."

"Gillian, how much time do we have?" Mandy asked, biting her lower lip.

"A couple of days. Maybe hours. My parents didn't expect an earthquake this soon. It will change the timing."

* * *

Gillian and Mandy walked side-by-side silently toward the main lobby. When they rounded the corner, Gillian was shocked. Half the students, who'd been there an hour before, were gone. The remaining kids slept, listened to MP3 players, or read like it was any other meet. "Umm, where is everyone?" she asked a boy coming out of the bathroom.

"A bunch of teams left a while ago to go home. The rest of us are waiting for our coaches to come from the hospital."

118

Mandy found a blanket and pillow while Gillian looked for a comfortable spot to sleep. They made a bed in a corner and soon P.J. joined them.

"You ever have a sleepover at your school?" Mandy asked.

"No," Gillian and P.J. responded in unison.

"I always thought they were fun."

Chapter 20

Johnny rounded the corner as Derek entered from a dark hallway on the opposite side of the cafeteria. He couldn't believe what he'd heard. He busied himself folding blankets. He hadn't been able to meet Gillian's gaze.

Mandy was lying on the floor. "Mandy, your brother." He nodded in Derek's direction.

Mandy stood. "Where have you guys been?"

"Never, mind it doesn't matter," Derek interrupted before they could answer. "Did you find anything?"

They were silent.

"Well, I did. Come see." Derek led them down the dark labyrinth of school hallways. The farther they walked the quieter it became. He stopped at the school shop where a car sat on blocks. "I've had enough. I'm going home."

"The coaches won't let us leave. Besides we don't have money for gas and who knows what the roads might be like," Johnny argued.

"I'll worry about all that when I get the car running."

"I'm in." Mandy walked away. "Let me know when you're ready to leave."

Johnny ran a hand through his hair. "I'll help. But you have to drive me to the hospital when we get it fixed. I need to see Wesley."

"Let's do it then."

March 18th

Chapter 21

Bridget Turner woke to the gentle shaking of her husband. "It's time," he said. He handed her a piece of fruit and a protein bar. The bags that sat on the floor in front of her were gone, as was the teddy bear. "Ready?" he asked.

Bridget nodded. She turned before she closed the door behind her and said a gentle goodbye. Outside, the air was crisp and Bridget found her lungs aching. Cal had the truck already warm and she eagerly hopped in. "Oh, my gosh, this feels like heaven," she told her husband.

"I know. The temperature really dropped last night. "Cal put the truck in reverse and pulled out of the driveway.

Dawn's pink promise had yet to appear as they drove down dark streets, wary of animals. Where the night before Cal saw many people wandering the streets, now the town was empty of life. Bridget felt guilty as they headed north toward the airport. They pulled in, parked and met Nash at the tarmac.

"Good morning," Nash greeted them. "What a night. Have you heard anything?"

"Nothing," her husband said as he shoved their bags into the copter.

"Yeah, my wife still can't get our emergency radio going. I told her to head over to the hospital. I wonder if it's just us in the valley."

Cal shrugged and helped Bridget into her seat.

"Ready?" Cal asked.

Nash nodded and they both got in.

"I spoke to the air traffic controller. He's had no one fly in since last night and he thinks everything is grounded, but he's not sure. I told him getting you out was of vital importance to the United States of America." Nash studied Cal's face.

"Great," Cal said. "Then let's get going."

"Casper, then Dulce, New Mexico. Here we come," Nash said.

* * *

Mandy woke at dawn to a strange sound. Derek lay close. She looked around, rubbing sleep from her eyes. Someone was at the front door of the high school shouting. Gillian stirred beside her.

"Gillian!"

Gillian turned in the direction of the noise. Tears streamed down her face. "Mandy, my mom and dad! They're alive," she said. Gillian rose and ran to the doors.

Mandy stood and, not sure if she should interrupt the moment, wandered over. Gillian pushed open the locked emergency door. "Mom! What are you doing here?"

Ignoring the greeting, Bridget instructed, "Say good-bye, Gillian. The chopper's outside waiting for us."

"Chopper? Why? How?"

124

"Never mind. We'll explain later."

Gillian obeyed. She turned to Mandy, hugged her, and whispered, "You have to go. Don't stay here. Time is running out."

Mandy quickly wiped away the tears that filled her eyes.

"I will," she said.

Mandy stared after Gillian and her parents. She wasn't sure what to do. Wake the boys? Find breakfast? Or tell someone? She stood stuck, contemplating each option. Finally, Mandy decided to wake Derek. She needed to know about the car.

Shaking Derek, she put her fingers to her lips, and shushed him. He blinked and rubbed his eyes. Mandy tiptoed away from the group with Derek following. They walked down the hall, through the cafeteria, and left the sleeping teenagers behind.

"Is the car ready?" Mandy asked.

"We didn't get much done last night. We looked under the hood. All the parts seem to be there. But we only had a flashlight. Why?"

Johnny, Trisha, and P.J. joined them. Apparently, Mandy hadn't been as quiet as she'd thought.

"Hey, what's up? Is this one of those secret sibling club meetings only brothers and sisters can be a part of?" Johnny sarcastically asked.

"Mandy was asking where we were with the car. I was telling her, when you interrupted," Derek snapped.

"Oh," Johnny said.

"Mandy?" Derek asked.

"What's going on?" P.J. added.

A tear slipped down Mandy's cheek. "Gillian's parents came and took her."

"What? When?" Johnny asked looking behind him.

Mandy could see the dawning realization of the truth in his face. "Like ten minutes ago."

"So, what?" Derek asked.

"I, um, feel scared. I want to go home. I'm worried about Mom and Dad," Mandy said. "I want to go now."

Derek hugged her. "It's going to be fine. I'll get you home." He hesitated and then suggested, "Why don't you and Trisha go get our things? I'll get the car ready."

Mandy nodded. The girls hurried back toward the cafeteria. "Do you think we'll get in trouble?" Mandy asked.

"Trouble? No, I think if anyone found out they'd just stop us."

"We can't let that happen. I have to get home," Mandy said. "I know, why don't you get a trash bag for us to put our stuff in?"

"Why?" Trisha asked.

"If we take our suitcases, people are more likely to notice. But if we put our belongings in trash bags, it will look like we're cleaning up."

"Okay." Trisha nodded.

Mandy sat in a corner with her back to the wall, so she could see anyone who came close. She opened her bag and removed essentials, putting them in one pile. She grabbed the little blanket she'd used the night before and shoved it to the side. She continued the process of searching P.J's, Derek's, and Johnny's bags, looking for anything of value. She was sad at the thought of leaving small treasures behind. Mandy never considered herself a keepsake kind of person, but she was

126

beginning to believe she was. Her favorite sweater and pair of shoes were in her bag. But there was no way she'd be able to get everything without someone noticing. She sighed and before she knew it, tears threatened again.

She grabbed wallets, watches, and MP3 players. She found candy bars, five bottles of water and rounded up all of their blankets. Mandy looked up to see Trisha coming towards her with two trash bags.

"I only could find these."

"I think it'll be okay," Mandy said.

"What do we do with the rest of our stuff?" Trisha asked. "Aren't people going to become suspicious if we leave things behind? We should get rid of it. Make it look like we were never here."

Mandy blinked. Trisha was right. She looked around.

If they relocated their stuff to other people's piles, it would blend in. Mandy picked up a bag, quietly walked towards the closest sleeping group and set it up against the wall with a pile of other bags. Trisha followed her lead and in a few minutes, they were done. They exited the cafeteria with their backpacks placed in plastic bags. Mandy looked over her shoulder. If anyone came looking, it would be as if no one was ever there. Their little group had disappeared in less than five minutes.

They hurried down the corridors toward the shop where the car waited.

"I'm so scared," Mandy said.

"Yeah, me too," Trisha told her, "and cold."

They entered the garage and found Derek and Johnny at it.

"What do you mean, we can't tell anyone? We have to tell a coach. What if someone comes looking for us?" Johnny demanded.

Derek took a step towards Johnny, and grabbed the front of his shirt. "You won't tell anyone. My sister and I are going home. If you tell, they will try and stand in our way. If that happens, trust me, someone will get hurt."

"What if your parents come looking for you? What if your coach comes looking for you?"

"They won't."

"Derek, Johnny has a point," P.J. said. "If my parents showed up, I'd want them to know I'm headed home."

"Then stay and wait for them."

Johnny looked up to the window. Mandy's eyes followed his. The sun had risen and now put a streak across Derek's contorted face. She knew Johnny wasn't one to back away in a fight, but she sort of hoped he would this time. Johnny shook his head.

"I'm going to tell Coach. I'm not going to lie."

Derek placed his palms on Johnny's chest and pushed. "I want you to ask yourself if your girlfriend is going to still like you when I ram my fist in your nose."

Johnny shoved him back. "Trisha will like me no matter what happens here."

"Really? Should we ask her?"

Johnny turned to see Trisha and Mandy standing in the doorway.

"My sister will stand by me no matter what. Ask yourself, will Trisha do the same? I have the keys. I found the car. I fixed it and I'm in control. So I make the rules."

128

"Derek, stop it," Mandy demanded, running to him. "We need to get out of here before someone comes."

"How about I break your face and you can catch a bus to the hospital instead of going home?" Johnny said through clenched teeth.

"How about I just leave you here?" retorted Derek.

Johnny shoved Derek one last time and walked to Trisha, grabbing her hand. He led her to the car. He opened the door and she climbed in. Johnny looked at P.J. "You on his side?"

"I'm not on anyone's side."

"So what are you going to do?" Johnny asked him.

"I need to get home. I can't hang here forever. I'm not even sure where my parents are."

Mandy saw Johnny's back stiffen. "How do I explain to my coach how I got to the hospital?"

"You're sniveling," Derek said.

"I'm just saying, I feel bad lying to him. I understand you want to get your sister home. But look at it from my perspective."

"Get in the car. We don't have time to debate this any longer," Derek hissed. "We need to go. When I drop you off, give us a head start. Then you can tell your coach anything you want."

"The Pontiac's fixed already?" Mandy asked.

"It needed an oil change, but it looks like they never got around to doing it. All the parts are there, we put the pan back on, and lucky for us it has a full tank of gas. Now let's go people, before we get caught."

"Isn't someone going to notice a car rumbling out of the garage?"

Mandy could tell Derek was growing impatient with her questions.

"This garage is at the back of the school. I'm going to open the door, drive across the football field and onto a back road. We should be fine."

The rest of the group hopped into the car, bags squished between them, while Derek opened the door. Light streamed in. Mandy blinked, her eyes adjusting. From the front seat, Mandy saw Johnny grab Trisha's hand and hold it tight. They didn't shut the garage door behind them.

Johnny leaned his head against the seat. "Anyone have any ideas how to tell our parents we just stole a car?

Derek glared in the rear view mirror. Mandy watched as Johnny tucked Trisha next to him.

"So, Derek," Johnny said a few minutes later. "You might want to stop driving like you're in the Indy 500. You'll either kill us or get us pulled over."

"Shut-up," Derek said through clenched teeth. "Or I'll kick you and your girlfriend out and you can walk."

"You're a jerk. I can't believe you and Mandy are part of the same gene pool."

Derek swerved toward the curb.

"Derek, don't," Mandy pleaded. "Just let it go."

"Maybe I should rearrange your face," Derek hissed turning in his seat.

"What is your problem with me?" Johnny asked.

"You're full of it. You're the guy who suckers people in with your quick wit and smile. Until the wind changes; that is. Then you drop them. Wesley, who is supposed to be your best friend, needed you, yet you went off chasing a girl. You left

130

him high and dry. That's my problem with you. No girl or speech partner should be hurt by a piece of crap like you."

Johnny opened his mouth as if to say something but quickly closed it.

"Johnny did what was best for Wesley. You don't know all of it. You don't know their history," Trisha defended him.

"I don't need to know. But I'll tell you this. If he did that to me, I'd never forgive him."

"Stop," Mandy yelled. "We could all die and this is what you're doing?"

"We're not going to die, sis. We're okay."

"Leave Johnny alone."

Johnny touched Mandy's shoulder. "It's okay. We'll stop."

They sat in awkward silence, while Derek drove on.

Two blocks from the hospital Derek pulled to the side of the road. "Okay, here you go," Derek said.

"What do you mean here you go?" Johnny asked.

"I'm not pulling up to the hospital parking lot. That's asking for trouble. If your coach, or any coach for that matter, sees us, they'll wonder what we're doing. My sister won't be able to get home, which will then make the whole process of stealing a car a pointless endeavor. So, again I say, your ride ends here." Derek watched Johnny in the rearview mirror.

Johnny's lips curved up and his brows furrowed together. "Look, it's freezing out there. You could at least drive us one more block. You'll have plenty of time to get away before anyone notices."

"Aren't you from Riverton? Quit being such a wimp."

"Trisha and I don't have winter coats on."

"Fine." Derek slammed the car into drive and squealed the tires. He moved several yards before stopping again.

"Gee, thank you," Johnny said. He reached for the door. "I can't believe you guys are going to drive away like this. What kind of people are you?"

Johnny climbed out with Trisha behind him. He barely shut the door when Derek peeled away from the curb.

"Come on, Derek. You don't have to be so mean, Mandy said.

Derek didn't answer.

* * *

Mandy turned in her seat. P.J. had sat quietly in the back seat of the bouncing car. It seemed they'd been driving forever. He hadn't moved or said a word since they'd dropped Johnny and Trisha off at the hospital. Mandy figured he didn't want to make Derek angry, and possibly be the next one left on a curb. He was as anxious to get home and see if his parents had tried to contact him as they were to get to Shoshoni. So she was startled when he asked, "So, Derek, what's Shoshoni like?"

Derek scoffed. "Like any small town with cows."

"Oh."

Mandy could see it wasn't quite the insight P.J. had hoped for. He stared back out the window. "Tell me about your mom and dad. You guys close?"

"Um, what?"

"Your parents. Do you get along with them?"

132

"I'm trying to drive through snow, on icy roads with debris, and potholes the size of a cow's head, and you want to get touchy-feely? I think we should do this another time."

Mandy turned to face P.J. "Yeah, he gets along with our parents. They own the Shoshoni ice cream shop." Derek glared at her, but she kept talking. "You know, the one everyone in Wyoming has been to." She grinned. "We have the most wonderful ice cream. Heaven in a little cone."

P.J. nodded. Maybe if the two of them talked the tension in the car would go away. Derek hit a bump and both her and P.J. slammed their heads on the roof.

"Damn, there are so many potholes," Derek grumbled.

P.J. slid down in his seat as if to protect his head from the next set. Mandy felt uneasy.

"Wow, this road is crazy," P.J. said. "Is this part of the state having a budget crisis?"

"It's never looked like this before," Mandy stated. "And have you noticed all the animals are gone? I've seen nothing. No birds. No deer. Nothing."

Mandy leaned over to look at the clock. They'd been driving for forty-minutes.

Derek pulled over. On their right, they overlooked a giant lake.

"Where are we? Where did this come from?" Mandy asked.

Derek pointed to the sign that read, Shoshoni 20 miles. He stepped out of the car. "Maybe the dam broke when the earthquake hit."

"Sure is a lot of water," P.J. said.

"There's never been water here before," Mandy told P.J. "It's normally a huge field."

They both followed Derek to the water's edge.

Looking toward the east, P.J. sucked in air. "Look." He pointed. Thick black smoke covered the horizon. "Guess, I'm not going home anytime soon," he said.

Mandy shook her head. "Doesn't look like it. So what's your plan now?"

"I don't know. Maybe Gillian was right. Perhaps we should leave and go to Alaska or Arizona."

"What are you talking about?" Derek asked.

"Gillian told us the Yellowstone volcano is going to blow." P.J. snorted. "She and her parents are going to colonize Mars. She said the only safe places might be a bio-dome in Arizona or going to Alaska. Both are far enough away to be out of the initial blast zone."

"That's crazy." Derek shivered and pulled his coat closed.

"I called her a fruitcake when I heard," P.J. said. "But I think I believe her now. This is not normal. If Yellowstone is going to blow, I'd rather not be close."

"Mandy, we have to get home," Derek said.

They jumped in the car.

"I can't believe what is happening," P.J. said. "I wish I had cell phone reception. I'd like to call Sherry. Or my parents. I hope they are all okay." He lay back against the seat and closed his eyes.

"Me too. Do you know where your mom and dad are?" Mandy asked.

"Yeah. They're in Malaysia. "

"What are your parents doing in Malaysia?"

"Helping people. They travel a lot."

"Why don't you go with them?"

134

"I did for a while, but it got too dangerous. One time, in a remote village in Tibet, we awoke to shouting. People were running in every direction. Men with guns held people hostage, shouting orders and threatening to shoot. My parents cut a hole in the back of our tent and we escaped into the mountains. After that, we came back to the States and stayed for about a year. Then one day a nanny showed up at the door and my parents were gone again. When I was ten, they asked me if I wanted to go with them, but I had friends and sports. I decided to stay home."

Derek sped up.

"Listen, I have family in Alaska. Why don't we head there after we find your parents?" P.J. asked.

Derek looked hesitant. "I'll discuss it with them. See what they think."

Silence descended and Mandy focused her thoughts on her parents. She hoped they were okay.

Thirty minutes later, they pulled into Shoshoni. They drove down Main Street toward the ice cream shop. It had taken them twice as long as it should have, but Mandy was just happy they'd made it.

Mandy looked down the block, stunned.

Derek stopped the car in front of their charred shop. Smoke curled into the air and drifted on the breeze. "What the – ?" Derek said.

Mandy blinked back tears, her mouth opened as she gulped in air. A man on the street ran toward them. Mandy rolled her window down.

"Derek, Mandy." The man stuck his head into the car. "We tried to call you. Thank goodness you're here."

"What happened?" Mandy stammered.

"Don't know exactly. But your parents are at Doc's clinic."

Derek ignored the rest of what the man said and roared away.

Mandy sobbed. "Oh my God Derek, what if they are hurt? What about the shop? What are we going to do?

At the clinic, all three climbed out and headed up the sidewalk. People sat everywhere. It seemed as if the whole town was gathered. A woman stepped close to say something to Derek, but she teared up, turned and walked away. Another man mumbled, "I'm sorry," as they passed.

Chapter 22

Derek opened the door to the doctor's clinic and held it for Mandy and P.J. The lobby was as cluttered with people as the front lawn. Mandy took a step back, overwhelmed with the sight of so many injured. The doctor rushed by, but abruptly stopped in front of Derek.

"You're here! Good. We've been trying to get in touch with you."

"What's going on?" Derek asked. "Someone said our parents are here."

Mandy held back a sob.

"Let's step into my office."

They followed him through the sea of people.

"Doctor. Doctor, I need to have the ...." A nurse stopped talking when she saw Derek and Mandy. "That's okay. I'll figure it out." She rushed off in the other direction. They walked through a set of doors and stepped into an office to the left.

"Your parents were caught in a fire at the ice cream store. I could mince words, but want to be honest. I'm sorry, but they're not going to make it," the doctor blurted "We've made them as comfortable as we possibly can. They're in bad shape and with the roads being so damaged and all, we aren't able to get them out to a burn unit. I want you to be prepared. We are hoping the National Guard will be here soon."

"What?" Derek demanded.

"What happened." Mandy's voice shook and she suddenly felt unsteady

"Listen, I've got a dozen other patients I need to tend to." The doctor headed for the door. "Didn't your mom have family back east? It's crazy right now, but even in natural disasters protocols must be followed. I'll need to advise social services. They'll take care of you until arrangements are made."

Mandy sobbed in Derek's arms. She still couldn't wrap her mind around what was happening. "Derek?" she pleaded, not really know what she was asking for.

"I'm eighteen," he said. "I'll take care of her."

"Listen, I'm not going to argue with you. I've got patients everywhere who need me. I'll let social services and the courts sort it out."

Mandy couldn't speak. Everyone was talking like her parents were already dead. Tears streamed down her cheeks. Derek pulled her closer, his own eyes damp.

How would she survive without her mom and dad? And they'd take Derek from her too? Who would be there for her? Talk to her about boys, and make her feel better when her heart was broken?

"I'm sorry. I have other patients to check. Your parents are in the room at the back of the office. I'll come as soon as I can."

P.J. stepped closer and looked down at Mandy. "This is crazy. You guys, I can't stick around. I'm an emancipated minor, but I don't have papers on me. I need to go. And I think you both should come with me right now."

138

Mandy looked at him in disbelief. "I can't leave now. My parents . . .I'm not leaving my parents."

"You heard the doctor. They aren't going to make it. And he's going to inform social services. I don't want to be cold, but say goodbye and let's head out before Yellowstone erupts."

"Are you out of your mind? Those are my parents. I'm not leaving. You don't know them. They're strong. I'm not giving up hope," Mandy said.

"P.J., Mandy is right. We need to stay here for now. How about we meet up with you in Alaska? We'll head out as soon as we can." Derek said blinking, his voice strangled.

"My family lives in Anchorage. They own the B and B Inn," P.J. said. "Can I take the car?"

Derek shrugged. "We'll take my parent's truck when it's time. Here." He handed P.J. the keys.

There was an awkward moment. No one knew what to say or do, finally Mandy stepped forward and gave P.J. a hug. "You be careful."

Following Mandy's example, Derek also gave P.J. a hug. "We'll see you soon," he said.

"Yeah, I'll be waiting for you." P.J. seemed reluctant to leave, but Mandy nodded and walked away.

* * *

Mandy couldn't believe what was happening. She headed to her parents' room. She stopped short of the doorway and looked in. Tubes were attached to IVs in their arms. Mandy choked back a sob as she walked between their beds. The smell of burnt flesh rose to her nose and she gagged.

Taking a deep breath she looked at the stained ceiling. She thought about the last mundane doctor's appointment. A simple physical to make sure she was healthy enough to play basketball. She had no desire to play. She wasn't good at sports, but her parents thought it was something she should do. Just like staying beside her parents was something she should do. Mandy touched the bed-rail to steady herself. Derek came in behind her, blocking the exit.

"Doing okay?" A nurse walked by and stuck her head in the door. Derek nodded. "Here are your parents' things. Doctor asked me to give them to you." Then she turned and scurried away.

Mandy took her parents wedding rings from Derek and slipped them on as she stepped closer to her Mom's bed. She started to touch her hand, then pulled back. Her mom looked so tiny wrapped in bandages from head to toe. She began to cry again. "Mom," she moaned. The machine next to her mother stopped beeping. Derek and Mandy looked at each other. Her sobs grew louder.

"You didn't do anything," Derek assured her. "I bet she was holding on until we were here. I'll get Doc."

Mandy stood unable to move. The doctor rushed in with the nurse close on his heels. He pushed Mandy to the side. They checked the machine and nodded to each other, then quietly backed out of the room.

"Give them five minutes. After that, we need the bed," She heard the doctor tell the nurse.

Mandy looked at her feet. She didn't know how to say goodbye to her mother. She leaned over, tears creating a small stain on her shirt. She choked on her words, looking from her

140

mother to her father. Before she could gather her wits, two nurses entered, and wheeled the bed away.

"I'm so sorry. We need the bed," the doctor said from the hallway.

"What are you going to do with her?" Derek demanded.

The doctor shook his head. "We've had a number of casualties," he said not answering the question.

The wheels made a hollow thud all the way out into the hallway. Mandy turned to follow, but Derek stopped her.

"Don't make it worse."

Derek held his sister close as she cried on his shoulder. "I know," he said. "I'll protect you." Mandy looked at her brother. "Go to Dad. Don't worry."

"I killed…"

"No, you didn't. Mom let go because she knew you were here and safe. Let Dad know you're okay."

She went to her father, tears spilling over her lashes. Her voice caught in her throat. She stood, lightly touching his hand, and prayed he'd be okay. She couldn't lose them both.

Chapter 23

P.J. pulled into Fromberg, Montana and gave a huge sigh. The road had been rough, filled with potholes and cracks. He'd found himself spending half his time making sure he didn't break an axle or find himself stuck. Now, exhausted, all he wanted was to find a place to sleep. He'd driven past several motels on the way, but always the signs read, "Closed," and the doors were locked.

The sun lingered on the horizon, and as he drove into town, he noticed no lights burned from the homes. The power outage from the earthquake was more widespread than he'd guessed. He drove slowly, his eyes searching for signs of life. Then he saw a flickering candle set in the window of, he couldn't believe it, a bed and breakfast.

P.J. parked the car. The cold air made him shiver as he walked to the front door. He rang the bell and straightened his clothes. He ran his hand through his hair right before the door opened. A grizzled old man looked P.J. straight in the eye.

"What do you want?"

"I, uh, notice you're a bed and breakfast. I'm looking for a place to stay," P.J. said. Behind the man, stood an older woman with gray hair and glasses. She tried to peer around her husband. P.J. smiled at her.

"Son, I don't think this is the place for you," the man said. He started to close the door.

"Wait, I have money and I really need a place to stay. Just for tonight."

"Cash?" the man asked.

"Um, I have credit cards," P.J. stated.

The man squinted at him. "How old are you, son?"

P.J. swallowed, straightened his back and lied. "I'm twenty. It's the credit card my parents gave me to use at college." He saw the man waver. "Please, I've been driving all day and I'm exhausted."

"Oh, Frank, let the young man come in. If he wants a place to sleep and he doesn't mind that the power is out, why do we? We can rub his credit card like we did in the old days. We don't need the machine to work. Come in," his wife said, pushing her husband out of the way so P.J. could enter. "You must be frozen," she stated.

In reality, P.J. had been quite warm in the car until he got out. Now inside, he realized how cold it really was. Logs burned in a fireplace. "Come sit by the fire. Have you eaten anything?" the woman asked.

The man followed his wife while he appeared to cautiously watch P.J. with hooded eyes.

P.J. had to think when he'd last eaten. "It's been awhile," he finally admitted.

"Let me get you a sandwich," she offered.

"I don't want to be any trouble," P.J. replied.

The man's eyebrows rose. "It's no trouble," he said. "Come and sit down by the fire. And Harriet, perhaps you should bring a couple of those chocolate chip cookies you have hidden away, too."

The Lords enjoyed sharing their home with the few tourists who found their way to town. Frank told P.J., "Been doing this for a few years. It was Harriet's idea." He shrugged. "It brings in a few extra bucks here and there." P.J. thought the couple seemed really nice.

"I've put you in the last room on the left," Harriet said as she came downstairs and joined them. "I got the fire in your room going for you, so you should be comfortable. I can't believe we don't have power yet," she said.

"Thank you again, for everything," P.J. said, rising from the couch. "It's just so incredible. The earthquake and then the power outage."

"Oh, we've seen our share of power outages and natural disasters. They always seem to work out in the end so don't you worry none. And we love sharing our home with such a nice young man," Harriet said.

"Well then, I'm going to turn in."

P.J. climbed the stairs and found his room. The fire had just been started and hadn't had much time to warm the room, but P.J. was sure the thick down comforter on the bed would help keep him warm. Candles burned around the room giving off a dim light. He wandered into the bathroom and washed his face. The icy cold water shocked him. Drying off his face and hands, he wandered back toward the fire. The nice couple downstairs had been fooled. He knew he wasn't the wonderful college student they thought he was. Instead he was a thieving high school student. He hated that he'd had to siphon fuel from cars because the gas station pumps weren't working. Yet, what were his choices? He shook his head.

Light flooded the room when the power suddenly returned. P.J. blinked several times, shielding his eyes, excited for electricity. Across the room, a radio's static filled

144

the air, interrupting his thoughts. P.J. went to turn the radio off. Then the static changed and a voice came from the box.

Chapter 24

∞

∞-We are in position,- ∞ Soluma-Rah transferred her thoughts.

Bodha, visibly distraught, acknowledged. ∞-Have you any thoughts of Ka?- ∞ he inquired. ∞-I worry he left so easily. It is not in the nature of his Beings to behave as such.- ∞

Soluma also worried over Ka's unproblematic departure. ∞-We've had no thought transfers. His ship is no longer in the area. We should proceed. Ka knows the council will not tolerate aggression.- ∞

∞-I am most prepared, but I cannot ensure the Disposables will acknowledge our assistance and freely come with us. In the event they choose to arm themselves for conflict, I will no longer be of assistance to the council. This I must make clear. My Beings are concerned over the nature of what we plan. They are concerned we are intruding where we have no authority.- ∞

Soluma-Rah accepted all of Bodha's thoughts. When he finished, she waited the appropriate amount of ektons and then transferred calmly. ∞-Most High Bodha, you and your Beings know more than any other how our energy is connected to all other life, including the beings on the Water Planet. If they should perish, our galaxy's Beings shall feel it, sense it and will be discomforted. Your planet would then

146

know how we have failed. Perhaps many of your Beings already acknowledge the chaos Ka's decision to create earth movement made. I know my life force felt searing pain at so many being removed from the planet in such a way. We are here on a peaceful mission. One your Being should feel happiness at leading.- ∞

∞-I feel only disquiet,- ∞ Bodha thought sadly.

Soluma-Rah had noticed and felt Bodha's discomfort and understood his trepidation. They were all concerned over what to do. Her planet's officials had debated many moons before they acknowledged the wisdom keepers were right. Assistance must be offered. If only Beings on other planets had not used the Water Planet entities for testing. She knew on occasion Ka came to the Water Planet. He flew through the skies and created trails. He aroused the beings to fear. Since becoming Most High Elected, Soluma-Rah had many times thought to Ka about this breach of the treaty. Treating Water Planet beings like inferior energy was now what caused all of the evacuation team's concern. Creating more disruption on the planet would make matters worse. Their only hope lay in the council's help. Soluma-Rah felt a rush of emotion and cried out.

Bodha's thoughts intruded on her private ones, ∞-Most High Elected, what can I do for you?- ∞

While she knew he meant right now, at that moment when her Being was in such distress, she ignored her own pain and answered, ∞-We must save as many of the beings as possible. We must allow them to repopulate and thrive. You must lead us to this objective. Even then, I fear, we shall feel much sorrow, as we cannot take them all.- ∞

147

Bodha's image left her council chamber. Soluma-Rah, alone now, diminished her presence until she barely hovered over the floor of the ship. She spread out her limbs and felt the space beneath her, trying to draw energy from the rest of the Beings on her ship. She felt their life force willingly come to her in her time of need. She began to calm and the overwhelming feeling dissipated.

When, moments later, she drew herself back up, she was at peace. Soluma called to those who controlled her ship. ∞-We are most ready. Prepare.- ∞

* * *

Momur waited quietly beside Bodha during the entire thought transfer. Now Bodha turned to him. ∞-We shall proceed,- ∞

∞-The Most High Elected knows of your concerns?- ∞ Momur inquired.

Bodha affirmed. ∞-She knows and acknowledges. She fears the same. If her Being was from any of the other planets, I do not know if I would go forward, but of all in our Astral Zone, she is the one to be most trusted. Her thoughts are for amelioration. Her feelings showed clearly today. She is one with us.- ∞

∞-Soluma-Rah is not the Being to concern me. Ka and his Beings, Rohongra and hers. They are so willing to pick up their devices of purpose,- ∞ Momur continued.

Bodha accepted all of Momur's thoughts while his own private thoughts raced. How had he, in all the Astral Zone, become the one to lead this movement? Soluma-Rah knew his feelings. His planet had been the most reluctant to proceed

148

and now here he was, the face for what would occur to the Water Planet beings.

∞-I am most distracted Soluma-Rah asks this task of you.- ∞

Both of them, though, knew the reason. As peaceful Beings, they had mastered the movement of Ten-Dati. They above all the others would appear non-threatening. If there would be successful transference, it would be because of Bodha's peaceful image.

∞-Do you have everything ready?- ∞ Bodha inquired.

∞-All is prepared. The other ships have received the instructions for collection.- ∞

Bodha acknowledged. Momur's private thoughts begged the others to respect the instructions.

∞-We are here for a good purpose, -∞ Bodha thought.

∞-I wish for that,- ∞ Momur affirmed. ∞-The pulse is ready. It will cause the Water Planet's power modules to restart. They have a method of communication. It is primitive, but adequate. We've intercepted its waves and can recreate them. I have your shroud.- ∞ Momur slipped the diaphanous material over Bodha's shoulders. The shroud draped to the floor in soft folds.

Bodha's thoughts turned within.

∞-Our ships can assist with translation,- ∞ Momur continued to stream thoughts.

∞-Begin the thought transfer,- ∞ Bodha instructed.

Bodha cleared his vocal apparatus. He watched as his image coalesced on the screen in front of him. When he felt he was fully seen, he began.

"Beings of the Water Planet. Do not be afraid of my words. I'm Bodha, Most High of YonYa in the Astral Zone.

We have come in peace and with blessings." Bodha breathed deeply to calm his seldom-used apparatus. "Your planet is troubled and is no longer safe. This shall cause the deaths of many of your beings. As a Most High Elected and a member of the Astral Zone Council, I am to advise you our Beings feel the desire to assist your planet, and have devised a plan to aid." Bodha's thoughts searched for approval of his words. He instantly received it from Momur. A good friend, he thought.

"Your planet is losing life force. Many of your planet's power releasing land-sites are preparing for expulsion. When this happens it shall cause night for many of your moons. The dynamic movement you have felt recently is the beginning of this event." Bodha was not pleased to lie to the Water Planet, but he knew, as did Soluma-Rah, admitting one of them caused the occurrence would only worry the beings. "We are many Beings coming together to assist you and your planet. In our endeavor to do this, we shall, if your beings so wish, evacuate all of your healthy progeny up to the age you define as twenty-three. We shall only take those beings voluntarily and if your beings' leaders so wish. I must make this transparent to all. None will be taken by force, and if you, as a planet, choose not to evacuate your young beings, we shall leave as we have come, in peace."

Again, Bodha breathed deeply to relax. "You shall have one rotation to decide if you wish for our assistance. In two rotations we shall land our ships and begin transference. After our ships are filled to capacity or when no others so identified are wishing to evacuate, we shall leave. When we entered your orbit, we saw your energy systems and communication systems had failed. We have restored these and will continue to power them for you until the time when our ships will

150

depart your galaxy. Our Beings communicate naturally through thought transfer. When this communication is complete, the leaders of each of your countries should prepare to receive thought instructions for where collection sites will be located. That is all we wish to communicate at this time. May peace and blessings be upon you."

Chapter 25

Gillian and her parents crossed the tarmac and entered the large steel doors of the metal building.

"Hello. I'm Vincent Young." The commander of the Dulce, New Mexico base shook hands with her mother and father. "Dr. and Mrs. Turner. Welcome. Sorry for the security measures. I'm sure you understand. Right this way." He ignored Gillian as he led her family toward the elevator. "I wanted to come greet you personally. We weren't expecting you yet. We weren't really sure . . . Well, we can talk later."

The elevator doors closed behind them all. "You're the first to arrive since the quake. Do you have any information?" he asked as the numbers above the door decreased from twelve.

Gillian's dad shook his head. "Nothing new. We left Jackson as soon as the weather allowed. We've not heard anything. What news do you have?"

Captain Young seemed lost in thought for a moment. "We've had communication challenges. Cell phones and landlines are down. We haven't been able to contact anyone outside the complex. I imagine, once power is restored here the rest of the flight team will move quickly to join us."

"You've no power?" Cal asked. "I'm concerned. Could we have lost electricity in the entire west?"

"It's not just here?" Young looked agitated. "It's probably good then we've moved up the flight date. Instead of April 1st liftoff, we're planning for a March 21st date."

"That's four days from now!" Gillian's mother sounded shocked. She had an arm loosely draped around Gillian's shoulders, but her grip tightened.

Vincent nodded. "If the Yellowstone timetable has moved up, we don't want to take any chances. Many of the colonists have been here working to get things ready. Actually there are very few who were still in the field."

The elevator doors opened and Vincent extended his arm to hold them. Gillian's dad stepped out first, followed by Gillian and then her mother.

"This way," Captain Vincent said. He led them down a long dimly lit hallway. Numbered doors sat across from each other, as in a hotel. Gillian looked up at the open-beamed ceiling. Large metal lamps, hanging from girders, glowed orange.

"We have the generator working, but we're keeping power usage to a minimum. These are the private rooms. I've put you and your daughter in a connecting room. Here you are." He opened the door to room 143 and waited.

Two twin beds sat in one room and in the other a single and a desk. "Meals are taken in the cafeteria. You can find food at any time of the day. It's down at the end of the hall. All of the living quarters are on level seven. On level nine, we have the control room. In order for us to be ready by the 21st we'll be asking everyone to help with duties. By morning, I'll have a schedule for you both," Captain Young informed her parents.

Gillian wandered into the room with the bed and desk. She flipped on the lights and more of the strange orange glow warmed the area. She sat on the bed. A stiff and itchy dark gray blanket was folded at the foot. Gillian lay down and closed her eyes. They felt so tired. After landing in New Mexico at noon, they had trouble finding someone to take them to the base. Once at the base, they had to wait for papers and checks to be done. Now, late in the afternoon, Gillian held on to her teddy bear and let tears slip from her eyes. Angry, she wiped them away. Stupid. She wasn't a baby.

"Honey, we're going to the control room. Will you be okay?" her mother asked from the doorway.

"I'm going to take a nap," she replied.

"That's a good idea. We'll be back in a couple of hours."

Gillian heard the door shut and footsteps walking away.

Her eyes closed but her thoughts tumbled.

When Gillian woke later with a headache, she heard a strange ticking and it took her a moment to get her bearings. She sat up and quietly made her way to her parents' room. The backpacks lay on the ground as they'd been left.

Gillian's stomach growled. She opened the door and walked toward the cafeteria. Long before arriving she heard the delighted squeals of kids. Entering the room, she was surprised to find several mothers and their young children. Everyone looked up for a second when they saw her.

One mother, her hair pulled back in a ponytail, smeared peanut butter on celery sticks. A small boy tugged at her sweater and whined. Another woman sat with her elbows on the counter, coffee in front of her. The third mother rocked a fussing infant. Her eyes were closed, as if praying the child

154

would sleep, and the fourth woman put a puzzle together with a group of boys.

"Well, hello there," Mother Number Two said. "You must be the Turner's daughter, Gillian?"

Gillian nodded and pushed back an errant red curl. The women were all tiny and Gillian felt awkward in their presence.

Mother Number Three opened her eyes and studied Gillian wearily.

"Would you like something to eat? Some celery?" Mother Number One asked.

"Thank you." Gillian wandered over to take a stalk from the plate.

"If you're really hungry, I think there's some sandwiches in the refrigerator. Help yourself," Mother Number Two said.

Gillian found a sandwich and a place to sit.

The boys were now racing around in circles, while Mother Number Four stretched and rose to join the women at the counter.

"So, we heard you came by helicopter. How did your parents manage that? We've not heard a thing from anyone," Mother Number Four stated. She grabbed a celery stick and crunched on it. The small boy still whined at the heels of Mother Number One.

Gillian shrugged. "I don't know. I guess because the pilot is a friend he was willing to bring us." She chewed on her index finger until she noticed the woman was staring at her. Gillian quickly put her hands in her pant's pockets.

"Bang, bang, bang." Two of the boys ran by and bumped into Gillian's chair. Mother Number Four screamed at them to play nicely. The boys ignored her and continued to be disruptive.

Mother Number Five arrived, pushing a stroller with three little girls. "Hey, sorry I'm late. I know it was my turn to make snacks."

Mother One swatted at the air. "No big deal. You can catch it tomorrow. Paige isn't here yet either. Late naps?"

Mother Five laughed. "Yeah, how did you know?"

"None of us can stand to wake a child," Number One explained to Gillian.

"How many children are there?" she asked after finishing her sandwich.

"There are eight families and twelve children total. I think there's only four high school age," Number One said.

"Do you babysit?" Number Three asked.

Gillian choked. The women rushed to make sure she was okay. Gillian thanked them kindly, accepted the water they thrust at her, and quickly hurried out of the room. She went back to her room, but her parents still hadn't shown up. Bored, she headed toward the elevator. Inside, she punched in level nine and waited while the elevator carried her up, thankful she was an only child.

Gillian checked her watch. She was surprised to see how late it was. Certainly her parents couldn't still be working?

Moments later the elevator doors opened on level nine. Gillian was shocked to be standing in the dimly lit control room. She'd expected to find herself in a hallway not in the center of the action. She searched the sea of people, for signs of her mother and father. She spotted them, as the lights sprang on. Gillian heard the whirling and whining of

156

electronics. At the front of the room, a bank of twelve televisions flashed on, snow raining across the screen.

"We've got power," someone said, stating the obvious.

Several people whooped and hollered. Just as Gillian reached her parents, the snow cleared and an image appeared. All eyes focused forward. Gillian looked up and then stood immobile.

"Oh, my God," someone said behind her.

* * *

Gillian stared at the book in her hands. The words held no meaning.

"Creep!"

"Jerk!"

She looked up. The children she'd been forced to watch were fighting. She stared at them for a moment before her eyes focused back to the words on the page.

"Aren't you going to do something?" the teen next to her asked. She'd learned his name was Hammond when they were told to stay in the cafeteria and watch the children.

"Huh?" she said, even though she'd heard what he'd asked.

"I said, why don't you do something?" He spoke louder and slowly enunciated each word.

"About what?" Gillian was furious her parents had forced her to babysit these brats.

The boy huffed. "Kids! Knock it off or I'll tell your parents!"

The two boys who had been arguing, looked over. The oldest one stuck out his tongue.

Gillian giggled.

"Not funny," Hammond said.

"I'm sorry. I shouldn't be like that."

"I understand. Everyone is freaked out," he said. "What did your parents tell you?"

"I was in the control room. I saw it."

Hammond nodded. "My mom is worried. She thinks this whole thing is messed up. The timeline keeps changing."

Gillian sighed. "Yeah, my mom is scared, too. She thinks the volcano is getting ready to blow. If it goes before we get into the air, it may cause problems with our liftoff."

"That might not be the worst thing," Hammond said.

Gillian studied his face then. "Oh, yeah?"

"Yeah. We aren't ready and now people are thinking of leaving the project."

"Leaving the project? I'd think with what's going on they'd be more convinced it's the best thing."

"Not everyone agrees. I guess parts of the project were on a need-to-know basis. People were more inclined to go when they thought it was for exploration. Now they know the world is ending behind them, they've decided it might be better to stay. Be with their families," Hammond said.

"That doesn't even make sense," Gillian said.

"I agree. Then there are all the others, who were not included on the roster and now know the world might end, who want on, but it's too late or they aren't good candidates."

They sat back and watched as the two young boys wrestled on the rug in front of the television. Behind them on the screen, a woman recapped the speeches.

"So what happens if they decide not to go?" Gillian finally asked.

Hammond shrugged. "It depends on who's going to stay here. There are some people if they don't go, there's no chance of survival. That's why we're sitting here babysitting while the adults are all in the next room battling."

"Do your parents plan to go?"

"We're going," Hammond stated. "My father is Captain Young. Dad takes this kind of thing seriously. You see, he was directly ordered to go by The President. So we're going. How about you?"

"I think we're going too," Gillian said.

When the door opened two hours later, there was still no additional news. The parents of the young children came to get them first. With her charges gone, Gillian debated about whether to go looking for her mom and dad. Hammond seemed content to wait. Gillian stood. "I'm going to head out," she told him.

"You shouldn't," he said. "They'll come here. Seems like your parents and my dad are either in agreement or are still arguing. Which do you think?"

Gillian was finished thinking about it. She wanted to go to bed.

Before she had a chance to answer, her parents entered. Hammond's father was right behind.

"Let's go," Captain Young said and nodded to her parents. "See you at 0-6 hundred." He and Hammond left down the hall together.

"You ready for bed?" her mother asked. Her eyes were heavy and her voice raw.

"Sure," Gillian said. She waited until they were in their room before she spoke. "So aren't you going to tell me what's going on?"

"Not tonight," her mother replied.

"But . . ."

"You heard your mother, not tonight," her father said wearily. "Go to bed."

Even after the lights were out, Gillian heard their urgent whispers.

Chapter 26

Johnny shifted as Wesley groaned. "I've got bruises on my bruises," he said.

Johnny nodded in agreement. On his left, Trisha lay with her eyes closed. Her head rested on his shoulder so he could see the palm-sized bruise on her cheek. Huddled on the floor in one of the hospital waiting rooms, they were exhausted. Their coach, Mark, had come by a few hours earlier to check on them and they hadn't seen him since.

"How's your head?" Johnny asked Wesley.

"It's still there. I can feel it," Wesley replied and winced.

Eighteen stitches now lay beneath the bandage around Wesley's head. Concussion, the doctors had determined. They said he was a lucky one. No broken bones and no problems with internal organs. All of which meant, the physicians were able to stitch him up and turn his care over to someone else, in this case, Johnny.

"I wonder how much longer until we can leave?" Wesley questioned.

It was the same question they'd all asked. Mark said as soon as the last of the team was medically cleared, they would head over to the high school to collect the rest of the kids and go home. There was only one girl left waiting for her broken arm to be set. It seemed whenever she was about to be called, someone else would come in with a more pressing emergency, knocking her back down the list.

"Thanks," Wesley said.

"For what?" Johnny asked.

"For coming back and staying with me. For getting me out of that restaurant. You're a true friend. I shouldn't have said such crappy things to you before." *

Suddenly, lights came on. They could hear the sound of machines restarting and pumps going. Across the room, the television popped on to a static-filled screen.

Well, at least now they'd have some T.V. to occupy their remaining hours. A sigh escaped Johnny's dry, cracked lips.

But then Johnny's gaze didn't leave the television until the creature's face disappeared and a static-filled screen took its place. All he could think was Gillian had been right. But now what? He turned to Trisha, her face still lifted, waiting for something. Moments later the network newscasters came on to talk about what happened.

"I don't believe it," Wesley said.

"Yeah, some kids fooling around. Boy, are they going to be in trouble," a man said.

Trisha opened her mouth to respond. Johnny quickly nudged her quiet and shook his head.

"It's a good thing, though, the power is back on," a woman in a red sweat suit said.

"What are we going to do?" Trisha asked, looking at Johnny.

"Do you suppose it was a young kid under that mask? I mean the head-size was not quite right. Or do you think it was computer generated?" the woman next to the man asked them.

162

Johnny shrugged. "Anyone thirsty?" he asked Wesley and Trisha, as he rose from the floor.

Both hurried to follow him down the hallway. Now that power was restored the floor gleamed in the bright light. At the vending machine, Johnny dug out his last few quarters.

"Okay, we need to think here. Whatever that was, hoax or . . . or alien, it told the same story as Gillian. She was telling us the truth," Johnny said.

"So we're in trouble," Trisha murmured. "I don't even know what to think."

"What about Gillian?" Wesley asked. Johnny quickly filled him in. "If that alien thing was real," Wesley began and then getting a look from Johnny, continued, "Well, if it was, don't you think based on what Gillian told you, we should go?"

"It's The President!" someone exclaimed from the waiting room.

Johnny led them back. The floor where they'd been sitting was now occupied, as was every other available space. They stood in the doorway and watched. Johnny's mind spun. How could this be happening? The President looked confident standing behind a podium at the White House. Johnny focused his attention and listened as The President gave a speech that consisted mostly of what Johnny considered double-talk. All too soon, The President was done and still no one in the room knew the truth.

"He knows doesn't he?" Johnny asked Wesley.

"Knows what?" Mark asked as he joined their group.

"Whether what was said is true or not," Johnny quickly said.

Mark glanced at the television. A young woman with bold blonde hair recapped and summarized what had been said.

"I'm sure when The President figures out what is going on, he'll be back to let us know. And if it was a terrorist attack on our technology, someone will pay."

Wesley's mouth hung open as he squinted at Mark. Johnny had never felt so stressed. He trusted Mark, but Gillian was adamant no one was supposed to know. He took a deep breath. "Mark, can I talk to you about something?" he asked.

Trisha grabbed his arm. "Johnny, we shouldn't be bothering him right now. He's got so much on his mind," she said.

"No, go ahead," Mark said. "What's wrong?"

Johnny pulled his arm from Trisha's grasp and led his coach away from the crowded room.

"Do you remember Gillian? She does poetry for Jackson?"

Mark nodded. "Was she hurt in the earthquake? She okay?"

"Yeah, yeah," Johnny said. He turned to see Wesley and Trisha following closely. "Anyway, her parents work for the forest service at Yellowstone. Last night she told us the same stuff as that . . .thing on the T.V., that Bodha guy."

Mark's attention was now fixed on Johnny's face. "What did she tell you exactly?"

He lowered his voice to make sure no one else heard. "She told us her parents had documented the Yellowstone volcano was getting ready to erupt. She said her family was being evacuated and we should get as far away as possible,

164

because that quake was probably a warning things were going to happen soon."

Mark turned to Wesley and Trisha. "She said all that?"

Trisha nodded, while Wesley stared at his shoes.

Mark looked back at the waiting room. People were crammed around watching the news.

"She didn't say anything about creatures from another planet," Wesley piped in, "but that doesn't mean they aren't real, too."

Mark wiped his face with both hands. "I don't know what to say. I don't . . ."

When he couldn't go on, Johnny nodded. "I know. I feel the same way."

"They're giving the locations of the collection sites," someone yelled from the waiting room. "The President must believe this whole thing is true. Oh my God!"

"No! That can't be," someone else countered.

"Then why do it?"

Johnny held his breath. It was really happening! It was all true.

Trisha sank to her knees, crying out, "Oh, no."

Johnny rushed to pull her into his arms. Her tears quickly wet his shirt.

"Casper," someone called. "They are coming here to collect people."

"Children, they are coming here to save the children," someone else corrected.

"What about the rest of us?" an older man asked.

In the background, the blond woman continued to speak, recapping and reciting over and over what Bodha had said, what The President had said.

"Johnny, I need you to gather everyone who wants to go home right away. I'm leaving in an hour. I need to get home. My wife and daughter," Mark choked. "I need to get my wife and daughter to safety." He walked away, leaving them to stare at each other.

Chapter 27

The President of the United States paced in an underground bunker, angry over the lack of information. It had been twenty-four hours since the power outage began and even though he'd been working around the clock, he still had no knowledge of what was going on. The door opened and a whoosh of air rushed in with a staff member who laid a blue privacy folder with the White House security logo on the table in front of him.

"This just came in from Yellowstone."

"Tell me what it says."

"There has been no significant change detected since the quake."

The President shook his head before letting it fall to his chest. "Useless," he whispered. He couldn't believe he lived in a country with so much technology and yet, here he stood blind and deaf, completely cut off from the world.

The President looked up to see his staff member retreating. "Don't you have anything else for me?" he asked.

"Sir, official or unofficial?"

"At this point, I'll take whatever you have."

"Well, sir, I've heard rumors each of the local governors have issued a state of emergency. There is concern over food and the ability to get clean water. Because of the cold, people are gathering in shelters. I'm told gangs are looting Washington. The troops are mobilizing. A few minutes ago someone arrived from Minnesota from the governor's office. He's in right now with the Chief of Staff, being debriefed."

"Thank you," The President said. He waved his hand to dismiss the staffer.

The large T.V. at his back flickered on. Static interrupted The President's thoughts.

"Mr. President," the door opened and an excited Secretary of State entered. "Power has been restored."

"Obviously," The President retorted.

As they both watched, a shadowy figure appeared.

The President and his staff listened stunned. What in the world? "Is this for real?" he asked the room.

"We are showing the location of the initiating signal is from outer space," said the Secretary of State.

"Could anyone, a hacker for example, make this happen? I mean, how positive are we that we've been contacted by alien life?"

"One hundred percent sure. No one has the kind of technology needed to pull something like this off."

They listened intently and then a flurry of activity surrounded The President as the Being's speech concluded.

"Mr. President, you need to address the people," the Secretary of State said.

"Is this all for real?" Will Gilbert, the Director of the CIA, asked. "I mean, could this really be happening?" He looked around the room, but nobody met his eyes.

"We need to take action, Mr. President, immediately. We need to alert our troops," said the Secretary of Defense. "We can't allow aliens to enter our atmosphere."

168

"What? But what if this is our only hope for saving our children? We know Yellowstone is going to explode. We know lives on this planet will change. We've been trying to figure out what to do for years now. Why would we do anything to jeopardize the continuation of our race?" said Sean Weston, the Secretary of Agriculture.

"You're crazy. Who would send their children with aliens to another planet?" Gilbert asked.

"During World War II many families opted to do just that. They sent their children here. I don't know how parents will feel about sending their children into outer space, but don't you think they should be given a choice?" Sean asked the room.

"No, I think we need to protect ourselves."

"Protect ourselves from what? They're trying to help us."

"Enough," The President said. "Get ready for a press conference."

"I'll get the Press Secretary and let her know you will be live in…?"

"Ten minutes. I need a moment."

The door closed, leaving The President alone. He wasn't sure if he was ready for this. He took a deep breath and squared his shoulders. Standing in front of a mirror, he adjusted his tie, checked his hair and cleared his throat. It was time.

* * *

"Good evening, I'm Jessica Renfro and this is your World News Tonight." The camera focused in tight. "Moments ago the nation heard Most High Bodha of the

169

planet YonYa." Jessica couldn't believe what she was saying. Of all the . . . she just hoped it wasn't a hoax and her career wouldn't reflect this one lapse in judgment. "This transmission occurred only seconds after power was restored." Jessica listened to the voice in her earpiece. "I have Michael Davis, our anchor, on the line from South Dakota. Michael?"

The screen in front of Jessica sprang to life and there was Michael. His face was drawn and his eyes drooped.

"Good evening. I'm standing here at what some of you may not recognize as one of our country's most impressive monuments." The camera in South Dakota panned out toward a towering rock flooded with lights from below. "What was once Mount Rushmore, has been reduced to mere rubble."

Jessica tried to keep her expression calm.

"We have been told the earthquake, an 8.9 on the Richter scale, was one of the worst in our nation's history. Buildings in the surrounding area have collapsed, leaving tens of thousands wandering in the snow looking for shelter from the cold."

The earpiece voice informed Jessica they needed to cut away. "I'm sorry, Michael, we have more news from our Washington D.C. affiliate. Susan?"

"Yes, Jessica. We've been informed the quake in South Dakota was one of several that occurred simultaneously around the globe. Already reports are coming in that The President is being overwhelmed with calls from the world's leaders asking for assistance. Russia, China, Brazil and Australia have already reported devastation and loss of life in the millions. Here in the nation's capital, we are facing our own devastation, as looters take to the streets."

170

"Susan, is there any word from The President?" The camera image turned upside down and whoever held it was running. Suddenly the camera went black and Jessica heard nothing but static. Forcing her lips into a grim line, Jessica continued, "We have lost contact with Susan, our Washington, D.C. correspondent."

Jessica paused. She wiped her palms on her skirt. She took a deep breath. "And what of the being who called himself Bodha? We have with us via satellite Dr. Eloy Cummings, a lecturer and author of, "*Do You Really Believe We Are Alone?*" and Stanford Astrophysicist, Dr. Molly Brown. What can you tell us about this . . . this entity?"

"Well, certainly it would appear, at first glance, this is nothing but a hoax. An elaborate joke using the airwaves to capitalize on the fact power had been cut to the world. In fact, it seems they were able to use the earthquakes as a means to their own end," Dr. Brown began.

"Molly, surely you don't really believe that? For years our own astronauts have witnessed UFO sightings. We know we are not alone in the universe," Dr. Cummings retorted.

"I will admit, whoever is behind this had a great costume, but really, how can anyone in their right mind believe aliens have come to," she made air quotes, "'assist us'?"

"Oh, I can believe they are here. Of that I have no doubt. And I, for one, wonder if they may have had something to do with the situation the planet is in. After all, it seems most convenient they arrive just after we have earthquakes on several continents that are some of the worst in this planet's history."

Jessica's focus turned back to her ear. "I'm sorry, Dr. Brown, Dr. Cummings, thank you both. I have received word The President of the United States is getting ready to hold a press conference. We will break away immediately when that happens. But first, a geologist in Yellowstone will give us the latest from there." A still photo popped up onto the screen of a young man wearing a backpack and surrounded by towering trees. "Robert Visilia?"

"I'm here."

"Robert, can you tell us, is there any truth to what the being, who called himself Bodha, said?"

"Jessica, there is. I've been studying the situation here in Yellowstone for nearly ten months now. While the government officials have been quiet, I've been trying to get the word out. There have been all the signs of an eruption of great magnitude here. You can learn more about my predictions at my website, www.visiliablows.com."

"Thank you, Robert. We'll go now to Dan on the street. Dan, what are the people saying?"

Dan stood at an intersection outside the station. The street behind him was deserted. Jessica watched as one of the camera men stepped up to the microphone. "I'm afraid," the cameraman said. "I'm not sure what to believe. I wish The President would speak." Dan turned and Jessica's own makeup person came into view. "Yeah," she said. "Is this all for real?" Behind them a car roared into view and then raced past.

"Back to you, Jessica."

"Once again, good evening, I'm Jessica Renfro and this is your World News Tonight." The camera closed in on Jessica's face. "Moments ago the nation tuned in as Most

172

High Bodha of the planet YonYa . . ." Jessica repeated, wondering if it was all a bad dream.

* * *

The President stepped into the pressroom and into the camera lights. A young intern handed him an earpiece and attached a microphone to his lapel.

"We go on the air in ten seconds," the young staffer said.

The President nodded, gathered himself and waited.

"Five, four, three, two." The cameraman pointed at The President.

"Good evening, my fellow Americans. I stand before you at a time of crisis. The only way we can get through this is to remain calm. I'm sure all of you have heard the previous broadcast. We are looking into the facts and will establish their validity as soon as possible. Please know we are working around the clock to create a plan that will work for all Americans." He quickly stepped away from the cameras.

"Mr. President," Gilbert walked up to The President and whispered, "Please come with me."

He followed his head of CIA into the adjoining conference room.

"What?" The President asked.

Gilbert pointed. "I thought you should see this."

The President turned to find Weston sitting at the table. The pen in his hand moved furiously across the page. The President's eyes locked with Gilbert's.

"He started moments after you began your speech. It's as if he's in a trance."

173

"What's he writing?"

Will handed him a sheaf of papers. "A list of cities. We think these are the collection sites."

"We don't have a choice," The President said, his face drained of all color, "we must share this with the people."

The President's news conference was brief and to the point. He gave information on the collection site locations, but really didn't go into any more information and didn't mention Yellowstone at all.

"The people deserve to know," Sean Weston argued when he was off the air.

The President stared blankly at him. "We gave them info on the collection sites. Wasn't that enough?"

"No, there are still those who need to hear it from The President's mouth. Remember, the fewer people on earth the greater chance of our survival as a race. Our underground bunkers are designed for minimal numbers. And quite frankly, we don't know what anyone is going to do. Scientists say they expect a two-year nuclear winter. And we don't have any contingency plan or survivability rates at this time. Plus we know other parts of the world are also experiencing the same type of events. "

"I understand," The President said.

"Mr. President, you have to tell families what is going to happen. They need to know this may be the only way for their children to survive. It might allow some to find peace and hope in this disaster."

"Excuse me," an intern from the back of the room spoke in a quiet voice.

"Yes."

174

"I have two children, I would want to know what my options are. You are the only one who can validate the situation."

"With all due respect, you guys are crazy," Gilbert said. "You would send your children with aliens? You don't know anything about them. Who are they?"

"I'm saying," the intern piped up. "I would like to know all of the facts in order to make the most informed decision possible for myself and my children."

"She's right. This information needs to be shared. The people can make their own decision. Please let the media know I will speak again in an hour. I need to consider all this," The President ordered.

Chapter 28

Mandy felt she could cry no more. She hadn't said a real goodbye and now her mother was gone. Mandy looked at her father. His face was unrecognizable, and his labored breathing told her how he suffered. She was torn. She wanted him to live, but she also knew that was selfish.

"Your turn for a break," Derek said as he came to stand beside her. "Go get something to drink. Wash your face."

"I don't want to leave. I'm afraid if I do, when I come back, he'll be gone, too."

"You heard what the doctor said. It could be a long night. Go." Derek pulled Mandy up from the chair. "I'll be right here."

Mandy nodded, and gave her father one last look before leaving. She pulled the blanket tighter around her shoulders. Passing the reception area of the small clinic, Mandy saw Dr. Christensen snoring on the overstuffed loveseat. A nurse fussed with a stack of charts. People had cleared out as night fell, going to their homes and fireplaces. Now she and Derek were the only ones left. She did as Derek asked and used the sink in the bathroom to wash her face. She pulled out a brush from her backpack and pulled it through her long curls. All the while though, she bit her lower lip. She cupped her hands below the faucet and drank the cool water.

She looked into the mirror. The person who looked back was a mess and almost unrecognizable. Her eyes were puffy and red, and there was a scratch along her temple she didn't remember getting. Mandy turned away from her image and walked out of the bathroom, careful not to wake the doctor as she tip-toed past him.

Mandy was about to enter her father's room when she saw Derek leaning over the bed. Her father's lips moved and Derek's face was intent as he listened.

"I promise, Dad. I'll take care of her," Derek told him.

The tears, Mandy thought had all been spent, now poured. She leaned against the wall and slowly sank to the floor. She quietly sobbed. She couldn't go in and face him. Not after what happened with her mother. Not now. She needed a minute to regroup.

A hand cupped her mouth and prevented her from screaming. She jumped, startled by the sudden contact. Derek held the index finger of his other hand over his lips. Mandy nodded, confused.

"Come," he instructed. He pulled Mandy to her feet. This time he led her down the hall away from the room, away from the reception area, and out the back door of the doctor's office. Mandy only stopped when she saw where her brother was taking her.

"Dad?" she whispered.

Derek turned and shook his head. "Come on. We've got to go before Doc wakes up or his nurse comes looking for us. They won't let us leave. They're determined to tell social services on us."

Mandy fought against legs that wanted to buckle. He's out of pain, she told herself. It's good. He's out of pain and he's with Mom. She forced herself forward toward home, all the while wanting to see her daddy one last time.

"What are we going to do?" she asked when they neared their house.

"I'll meet you inside. Grab as much food as you can and we'll get out of here," Derek said.

"What about clothes?" Mandy asked.

"We can't take much. Remember, we don't know how much time we have before Doc wakes and notices we're missing."

Mandy nodded. She ran upstairs and pulled out a backpack and duffle bag from her closet. She quickly threw a few of her things into the backpack, before dragging both bags to Derek's room. She added what she thought he'd want. When she came down she found Derek in the pantry with a large black plastic bag.

"I'm getting everything we can easily eat on the road," he told her.

"What about money?" she asked.

"I've got Dad's credit cards. Grab the piggy bank and any other money or stuff you think we can pawn or use."

Mandy left the bags and ran back upstairs. In her mother and father's room she grabbed their jewelry boxes. She was coming down the stairs when the power came on. The lights flickered once and stayed on. She heard the static from the television. Her parents must have had it on before the earthquake.

"You ready?" she called.

A strange voice filled the silent room. Mandy stopped and then cautiously moved into the living room. Derek stood transfixed in front of the T.V.

"What?" she asked.

"I don't know," Derek said and he stepped away so she could see the figure speaking.

Mandy and Derek listened to the weird guy's entire speech. The muscles in the face seemed to show through the skin, giving him a strange orange tinge. And his eyes, which were deep blue, stood out against his skin. The alien looked somewhat human and the whole time he spoke Mandy hadn't felt freaked out. They stood in silence, neither one sure what to say. It seemed like a big hoax someone was trying to pull. But who and why? Mandy and Derek heard The President come on a few minutes later to assure people things were fine. More information would be coming their way, but they didn't have any time to stand and wait.

"We need to leave," Derek said. "Now."

Mandy heard a car pull into the driveway. "Maybe, it's a....," Mandy started to say.

"Nope, it's the sheriff. Doc or the nurse must've told him."

"Just great. Don't they understand what's going on?"

"I guess not, sis."

"Well, we have to tell them. We have to get out of here."

"I know."

Mandy looked at the door and gauged whether they could get to the truck before the Sheriff knew what came at him, but there was no way. He'd pulled up right behind their vehicle. Mandy sighed, ready for the inevitable, when the knock on the door came. Derek opened it, while Mandy stared

179

ahead. Her life sucked, she couldn't believe in a few days she'd lost her parents, the ice cream shop, and her home. Now she might lose her brother, too.

"Hello Sheriff. We were packing a few things. Need to head out to our Uncle's house. I was able to call him. So Mandy and I will be on our way."

"Sorry Derek, that's not possible. You know the rules. We have to take Mandy into custody until he can come get her. Interesting that you spoke to him. I just tried the number you gave Doc. It's been disconnected. You need to come with me."

"Where are you taking us?"

"Just Mandy. I know you're eighteen."

"Well fine, where are you taking her?"

"Derek, I can't tell you that. Now, let's all be smart about this and not cause any trouble."

"Why can't I just take her?" Derek asked.

"Because the law doesn't work that way, son."

"The law? Are you crazy? Haven't you been listening to what's going on? Aliens are coming. The planet is dying. Who cares about the law?"

"I do, son. And soon whoever is behind that hoax will be caught. But right now I'm interested in getting Mandy to Social Services."

"This is unreal!" Derek hit the wall with his fist.

Mandy's eyes pleaded with her brother. She didn't want to leave him. She hated to be so afraid. She wanted, no, needed, to stay with the only family she had left. A bag sat at her feet and a small purse was slung over one shoulder.

"Since you're already packed, we can get going," the sheriff told her.

180

"I don't want to, and I'm not finished packing yet. If I'm never coming back, I want a few of my parent's things to remember them by." She turned on her heels and went upstairs.

She didn't hear her brother's footsteps on the stairs and assumed the sheriff wouldn't let him follow her in case they climbed out the window, which Mandy was currently contemplating. But without the truck, she wouldn't make it far and Derek had the keys. Mandy slammed bathroom cupboards stalling for time. She shut bedroom doors with a force that rattled the frames and then, ten minutes later, she stomped down the stairs, a sulking, angry teenager.

"Sheriff, you really need to tell me where you're taking her. It's not fair for me not to be able to contact my sister. I'm her only family."

"We'll let you know when everything is settled. Where will you be?"

"Here."

"Great! I'll contact you as soon as there's a plan. Come on, Mandy, no more stalling. The social worker is meeting us at the office."

Mandy hugged her brother. "Don't worry. I'll be okay." She smiled. "Just don't leave without me."

Derek shook his head. "Never, sis." The sheriff grabbed her backpack in one hand and took her upper arm in the other, escorting her to the waiting car. Before they reached it, Mandy pulled out of his grasp.

"You have to sit in the back," the sheriff said.

"I'm not a fugitive."

"Sorry, police policy. All non-official people have to ride in the back."

"Jerk." She climbed into the open door and threw herself on the seat.

Mandy looked back to see Derek wave at her. She wondered if he was waving good-bye. If he left her in this crap hole when Yellowstone erupted, she vowed she'd find him and haunt him forever.

The sheriff climbed into the car. "You're going to love the place where you're staying. We've already made arrangements. They are the nicest family. They live on a ranch and have two children."

Whatever, she thought, the ranch wouldn't be nice when it was covered in ash?

Mandy sank into the old worn seat, her body molding to the back. She didn't want to live on anybody's ranch. She closed her eyes and thought of the last time she'd seen her mother. A tear slipped between her lashes. Stupid earthquake. Stupid, stupid earth.

A few minutes later they pulled up in front of the Sheriff's office. A small lady with grey hair stood outside. She waved when she saw the Sheriff.

"That's Louise, your social worker. She is going to take you."

Mandy grunted. She knew who she was. He stopped the vehicle and let her out of the backseat. She looked down the street. There was no sign of Derek. A lump grew in her throat.

"Louise, this is Mandy. She doesn't talk much, but she's a very bright girl."

"Mandy. We've met before. Remember?"

"Yeah. Chocolate mint. Two scoops in a bowl."

"Yes, well I need to take care of a few paperwork things with the Sheriff and we'll be on our way."

182

The Sheriff held the door open for them both.

"I'll wait here," she said.

"No, you'll come inside," he told her.

Mandy harrumphed, looked down the street again, and stomped inside.

"Teenagers," muttered the sheriff.

"Oh well, I'm used to this," Louise said. "Have you been listening to the news?"

"Yeah. Boy, whoever is behind that broadcast is going to be in trouble. I bet they have the FBI and the CIA all over it. Who knows how they did it, but it's going to mean some major jail time when they're caught."

"But the earthquake," Louise said.

"Well, the earthquake . . ."

Mandy couldn't stand to listen anymore.

Chapter 29

"I don't see any reason to leave if they're collecting here," Johnny said. "We'd never get home and back, not with the road conditions. We don't even know if we can get home." "

"What about our families?" Trisha cried.

Johnny led them down the hallway of the hospital. They already checked three waiting areas and had yet to meet with any other kids from Riverton. "I bet they're all at the high school waiting for someone to pick them up," Wesley said.

"Probably," Wesley agreed. "I sure haven't seen anyone else."

Trisha rushed past and ran to a pay phone where she skidded to a halt. "We should call," she said.

Neither boy asked whom. They knew.

Wesley reached into his pocket and brought out some change. "Here," he said.

No one made the move to be first. "Come on," Wesley said. "Rock, paper, scissors?"

"No, Trisha, you go first," Johnny said.

Trisha took enough change for the call, and after sliding it in the slot, dialed her home number. Wesley jerked his head and he and Johnny strolled down the hall to wait a respectable distance away.

"What do you think your parents will say?" Johnny asked.

Wesley shrugged.

"How's your head?"

"Better."

That was the real question. Would Wesley be able to go with the aliens? The television had been specific, healthy people under twenty-three could be evacuated.

Johnny stepped closer to Wesley and moved his hair so he could examine the two- inch gash that had been sewed shut. "It looks pretty good actually. That doctor did a nice job, considering he only had a flashlight."

Down the hall, Johnny heard Trisha sobbing into the phone, "I love you, Mommy." Tears welled in his eyes. "Dang," he said to Wesley.

They looked away when they heard Trisha replace the receiver. Johnny didn't know what was taking Trisha so long, but he wasn't about to invade her privacy by turning around.

"Who's next?" she asked when she finally joined them. Johnny pulled her into his arms and she quietly sobbed on his shoulder.

Wesley walked toward the phone.

Johnny waited until Trisha calmed a bit before he asked, "What did your mother say?"

"She said to stay in Casper. To go with the aliens. Oh, Johnny! She doesn't know what to think, but if there's any truth to what's happening she wants me to have a chance at life. She says the roads are bad. No one even knows if they can leave town."

"She said that?" Johnny asked.

Trisha nodded. "I can't believe this is happening."

Wesley was quick to rejoin them. "No answer," he said. "Your turn."

Johnny held out his hand and Wesley dumped the remaining change in it. "Be right back," he told them.

The telephone rang only once before his mother picked it up. Her breath was ragged as she asked, "Johnny?"

Johnny smiled. "Yeah, it's me, Mom."

"Oh, thank heaven! Russell, it's Johnny."

Johnny heard the extension pick up and his father's deep voice. "Son, you okay?"

"I'm fine, Dad."

His mother's soft crying could be heard in the background.

"Are you still in Casper?" his father asked.

"When the quake hit we were heading back to the hotel. I'm at the hospital now, but I'm fine. Wesley got a bit knocked around but he's good, too," he said.

"I'm glad to hear that, son," his father told him. "Real glad. Have you seen the television or listened to the radio? You know about what's going on?"

His mother's cries were building in intensity.

"Yeah, that's why I'm calling, Dad. Coach is gathering up everyone who is going home."

"Uh, huh."

Johnny looked down the hallway. Trisha and Wesley were sitting on the floor, their backs against the wall, watching him. Johnny turned away. "I can come home," he said. "I'll be there as soon as I can."

"No, son," his father said.

"I love you," his mother rushed to add and then he heard the phone click as she hung up.

186

"Your mother and I talked about it and we want you to stay there. We don't know if all this stuff is real, but we do know you're safer there and if you can, if it's true, you should leave. We want the best for you. If we lived somewhere else, we'd not worry, but we're too close to Yellowstone. We're too close. The rumors say it's going to erupt. Well, it's way overdue. We figure if we'd have had more notice – well, I'm not sure more notice would have made a difference. Listen, save yourself. Do whatever you have to."

Johnny choked back the emotions that rose in his throat. "Dad, I love you. Please, leave and go north. Get as far away as you can."

"Oh, we'll try to leave right after we hang up. Won't we?" his father said, and Johnny knew his mother was listening to every word. "You've been a good son. I love you." Johnny heard the click and realized his father had hung up. He sank to the floor.

It was minutes later before Wesley came over. "I'm going to try my parents once more," he said.

His sigh a few minutes later said it all. "They should've fixed that landline. I've tried their cell phones, but the system must be overloaded. I can't get through."

Johnny wiped his face on his sleeve. Trisha still sat at the end of the hall, her head down. "Whatcha gonna do?" Johnny asked.

Wesley bit his lower lip and shook his head. He glanced at Trisha, then back to Johnny. "I don't know," he said. "I wonder what Mom and Dad are doing about my brothers and sister. Do you think they're on their way here?"

"Maybe." Johnny looked at his watch. "Listen, Mark is leaving in fifteen minutes. You don't have much time to decide."

The two boys walked toward Trisha, who rose when they were near.

"I'm going with you," Johnny told Trisha.

Trisha nodded and they walked through the hospital to the front waiting room. The coach from Casper sat in a chair whispering words of encouragement to a young freshman that Johnny recognized from the meet. "Have you seen our coach?" he asked when the man acknowledged them.

"Shoot, you kids just missed him. He left a couple of minutes ago. Said he'd gathered everyone who was going home."

Trisha's hands gripped Wesley's arm.

"Are you sure? He told us he'd be leaving in an hour. He sent us out to find any stragglers. I can't believe he'd do that," Johnny said.

The coach didn't respond, just chewed on something slightly offensive.

Wesley forced a smile. "Guess my decision was made for me," he said.

"But that's not right," Johnny yelled. "He shouldn't have done that. What if you or I or Trisha wanted to go home? He shouldn't have gone without us."

Wesley touched his shoulder and told him again it was all right.

They wandered the halls. Now that the electricity was on, it seemed even more people showed up for help. Soon, all the waiting areas were packed as crowds tried to see the latest news. All the beds were filled and each time Wesley, Trisha

188

and Johnny found a quiet corner, someone chased them out. Finally, they slipped into the back stairwell, huddled together and fell asleep.

March 19

Chapter 30

Gillian heard the quiet click of the door close and sat up. The clock read 2:00 a.m., she rose and went into her parents' room. It was empty. They'd only gone to bed an hour ago. Gillian knew where they'd gone. She threw on her jeans and a sweatshirt and slipped out the door.

With the power restored, the hallways were well lit day and night. The cafeteria on her left was empty, but she hadn't expected her parents to be there. She headed toward the elevator.

When the door opened on the ninth floor, Gillian stepped into the control room. Her parents turned and then went back to studying the computer screen in front of them.

"Thought you were asleep. We didn't wake you, did we?" her father asked.

"I couldn't sleep," she replied.

The computer screen held their attention. They had a second computer working on accessing information.

"What you doing?" she asked.

Neither parent seemed to hear.

"There it is," her father commented.

"Are you sure?" her mother questioned.

"Unfortunately."

Gillian strained to see the screen on her father's right. He pointed at some numbers that looked like coordinates. Then he used the coordinates to show a position on what appeared to be a star chart. "Right there," he said.

"What kind of window do we have?" her mother asked.

"We need to lift-off by 6:20 p.m. no later."

Gillian wanted to interrupt, to understand what they talked about, but she knew it was important. She waited patiently.

"Professor McMullen said he's not ready. The plants aren't loaded yet. He's worried he can't get it done by the 21st." Her mother grabbed a red phone from its station. "Captain Young, sorry to wake you. This is Bridget. You need to come to the control room right away." She hung up. Gillian's mother chewed on her lower lip.

"We'll make it work," her father said. "It'll be fine. Gillian, you should go to bed."

Gillian shook her head. "I can't sleep. Besides, I think I have a right to know what's going on. It involves me, doesn't it?"

Bridget Turner stepped to Gillian's side and gave her a hug. "You're right. Cal, let her stay."

* * *

"Okay," Captain Young said, "let me make sure I understand. The power we have is being facilitated by the aliens." Both Gillian's parents nodded. "And when their spaceships leave our atmosphere, you believe what the alien said – we'll lose power worldwide."

194

"Yes, and we don't know how long it would take, or even if we'd be able to restore it," her father added.

"And that might mean we wouldn't have enough power to get off the ground," her mother concluded.

"I don't know," Captain Young said. "That doesn't give us much time."

"I understand," Cal said, "but we have no choice. I've computed everything. If we have lift-off right at 6:20 p.m. the aliens will still be in range to give power, but hopefully focused on returning to their home galaxy so they won't notice our evacuation."

"That's pretty specific timing," Captain Young said.

"I'm well aware. Any sooner and they may think we're attacking them. Any later and we may not be able to get off the ground."

Captain Young scratched his brow. "The plants are the only things still not loaded. Professor McMullen wanted them under the lights for as long as possible before moving them. You heard him. He doesn't think they're ready."

"We have eighteen hours," Gillian spoke up. All eyes focused on her. "It's almost three in the morning."

"You're right." Captain Young shook his head and reached for the emergency call button on the console. "We'd better get going to make that deadline."

* * *

"I didn't expect to see you here," Gillian said. She dragged a large leafy potted plant from its row. She filled a dolly with them and took them to the ship.

"Every able body is to help," Hammond responded. "Didn't you hear?"

"Actually, I was sent here as soon as the Professor was told to get moving." Gillian and Hammond's heads turned to see the Professor, who was at the other end of the room throwing things around and muttering.

"He doesn't seem happy," Hammond observed.

"From what I've heard, he doesn't think we're ready, and leaving early means the project will fail," Gillian said.

Hammond bent down to help her lift the heavy pots. "In layman's terms, I believe he's saying we'll die."

Gillian almost dropped the pot.

"Easy," Hammond said. "He's probably exaggerating."

"Probably?"

They filled their cart and pushed it toward the ship's hold.

"The whole project is based on science from biospheres." Hammond pushed through the plastic flaps that separated the ship's plants from those still in the holding areas.

"Yeah, my mother told me some people, years ago, locked themselves up in a huge building in Arizona planning for this day. Only it was decades ago."

"Their enclosed project allowed eight people to survive for two years," Hammond explained. "They grew their own food and created their own oxygen. The problems they encountered have actually helped scientists know exactly what to do to recreate 'Earth' on Mars."

"Except . . .?"

"Except the time-table was moved up and some of the plants aren't quite ready. That means we may not have enough of them to sustain the colony of twenty-eight we're

196

sending. We might not have enough food fast enough. Or we could suffocate."

"Wow! I can't wait to go now that I know all that," Gillian said.

"Personally, I'm not worried."

"Oh, yeah?"

"Three reasons: One, scientists on these kinds of projects always have backup. Two, my dad's pretty smart and he's spent a ton of time checking everything. He seems to think we'd be okay. It's just more would be better."

"And number three?"

"Three: people are bailing out of the project. I heard before coming down here the family with the horrible tyrants, we watched the other night, backed out. Fewer colonists, less people fighting over food."

"Watch out!" Someone bumped into Gillian.

"Oink! Oink!"

"Hey, Tyson," Hammond said.

"You two know where I'm supposed to put the livestock? I've got pigs, goats, and the chickens are right behind me," Tyson said.

"You know where you're going with the plants?" Hammond asked Gillian. She nodded and pushed her cart to the left.

"This way," Hammond told Tyson. "Hey, Gillian, I'll catch up with you when I'm done," he called after her.

Gillian waved. "Okay."

She continued down the corridor and through two more plastic doors before finding herself in the agricultural area. Here, several more scientists were working. One was taking soil samples and waved her to the other end of the room, while another appeared to be measuring a leaf. Gillian stopped and waited until someone came by to instruct her where to place the pots.

They were much heavier now that she lifted them herself. She grunted and groaned and pushed and pulled to get each one lined up as closely as possible to the next. While she struggled, she saw other members of the team hurry to and fro with equipment and papers. Computers were fixed and wire connectors checked. Gillian stood and stretched her aching back.

She still couldn't believe this was happening. It felt creepy whenever she thought of the creature, that Bodha thing on television. While its orange face was thin, its eyes were huge. It reminded her of all the scary alien movies she'd seen since she was little. She believed if they hadn't planned to leave for Mars, her parents would've made her go to one of the collection sites. Which made her think of her friends from Wyoming. Would any of them go with the aliens? She hoped Mandy was safe.

"Get moving. There are more plants we need to get in here," the female scientist told her as she strode by.

Gillian felt like snapping. She'd wanted to help, but now she'd been working for hours and her stomach rumbled. "I'm going to go to the cafeteria and get something to eat," she told the retreating figure.

"You can eat now, or you can eat later," the woman said flinging her arm out to encompass the large room.

Gillian put her head down and pushed the cart back out to the holding area.

198

Chapter 31

Mandy sulked in the back seat of the social worker's red Subaru. Louise blabbed to Mandy about her new temporary family for twenty minutes. Mandy wasn't interested. She'd slept the night before in a local group home. Now they were moving her again. She kept looking in the rearview mirror waiting to see the familiar lights of the blue truck her brother always drove. But when she shifted in her seat to glance back, the road was empty. The earthquake hadn't done much damage on the west side of town, and as she looked out the window, she was surprised to see many people going about their daily business. Mandy crossed her arms and moved deeper into the seat. She couldn't believe everyone acted as if the world wasn't coming to an end. Didn't they pay attention to the news?

Now that power was restored, she wished she'd grabbed a phone charger. She could have called her brother on her cell and told him where they had taken her. She'd tried calling him from the group home, but wasn't able to reach him and only had one call. Quickly, she was losing hope she'd survive this disaster. She wondered how Derek felt. He was free to live how he wanted. He'd probably be enjoying life while she ate ash.

The car turned onto a dirt road barely wide enough for it. Potholes were everywhere and it seemed her prison guard had trouble keeping the car on the road. Ten miles later, they pulled into a driveway of an old ranch-style home with paint peeling, and a porch in desperate need of repair.

Mandy climbed out clutching her bag to her chest. A stout, hundred-plus pound, white dog came barreling at them full speed. Behind, a short rail-thin lady with out-of-control black hair and a drooling baby followed the happy dog. The dog knocked Mandy off balance and then jumped around waiting to be loved. Mandy reached down to caress the dog's head as a cat came sauntering around the house in the peripheral vision of the dog. The dog sprinted across the yard and chased the cat up a tree.

"Charlie, go." The woman with the child shouted to the dog while pointing to the porch. The woman took a step toward Mandy. "Hi, I'm Emily. You must be Mandy. And you've met Charlie. She's an American bulldog. This baby girl is Sasha. We're really happy you're here. Do you have another bag?"

"Lady, I'm sure you're nice. I love your dog. But don't expect me to get too cozy because I'm not staying here," Mandy said. Even she was surprised at her tone.

Mandy walked toward the porch to sit next to Charlie. She wiped at her eyes. She couldn't believe her parents were dead, or that Derek had left her. She sniffed. Louise made an excuse about Mandy's behavior, but Emily waved it off. Seconds later, Louise got in her car and drove away. Emily walked to where Mandy sat.

"I know you're not staying, but are you hungry?"

"A little," Mandy managed.

"You could come in, set your stuff down and have some lunch. I'll introduce you to the others."

200

"All right." Mandy stood and waited for Emily to enter the house first.

"Honey, this is Mandy," Emily explained.

A man with a long dark beard and scraggly hair turned around. "Hey. Welcome to the family. I'm Brad. This is Katy." He held up another youngster who was about five and dressed head-to-toe in pink baseball gear. They turned back toward the T.V. A news lady was recapping The President's speech.

"What a crazy thing going on in our world," Emily said. "It's a darn shame. Well anyway," she took two steps and entered a room off the living room. "This is the room you can put your things in."

Darn shame? Mandy had other thoughts. She walked through the doorway, took one look and placed her bag on the bed. Emily moved into the kitchen. Mandy could hear her opening cupboards and the refrigerator. She decided to join her.

"Can you cut those vegetables?" Emily asked.

Mandy grabbed the vegetables and the knife and begin chopping. If this had been her mom, it would've been nice. She smiled thinking about the first time she'd helped in the kitchen. She was nine and her mom was cooking her famous meatloaf. No one else had been allowed in the kitchen except for her. Mandy had washed her hands, put on a small white apron, and then told her mom she was ready for the secret. Mom laughed, her full-hearted laugh, and together they followed the recipe.

Tears trickled down her cheeks but she quickly wiped them away.

"This must be really hard for you," Emily said.

Mandy mumbled an incoherent response. She missed her parents, her home and her brother. A deep ache grew in the pit of her stomach. She hoped he'd save her soon. At least, when she was with him, it made life bearable. Without Derek, she didn't know if she could keep moving forward.

"What was your mother like?" Emily asked.

Mandy shook her head and kept chopping. She wasn't ready to talk about her mother to a total stranger.

"Okay, well, maybe another time. What do you like to do?"

"Hang out. Go for walks and work in my parents' ice cream shop."

"Oh, well, this is a big piece of property. You certainly can go for lots of walks. It's really pretty. There's a creek that runs through the back. In the summer we'll go tubing. It's lots of fun."

Mandy nodded and continued chopping. She didn't want to argue. Soon she'd be gone. Soon the whole world might be gone. Lunch was ready and Emily put everything on the table.

"Mandy, why don't you clean up and tell the others it's time and to shut off the T.V."

"Sure." Mandy walked into the other room. She stared at the television for a second until she realized the information the woman gave was the same stuff that had been said when Mandy walked through the room the first time.

"Um, lunch is ready. Emily says to shut off the TV."

Brad and the girls headed to the kitchen. Mandy heard Emily and him talking about the situation. He worried the aliens might be real and felt the situation was getting worse. Emily hushed him. Mandy went into the bathroom. Everything was worn, but not old. It was nice and smelled

202

like a home should smell, like lavender. Tears swelled behind her eyes again. Mandy stood staring at her reflection in the mirror for a while, watching the tears stream down her face. The terror of going on without her parents held her in place. She wondered if the hole in her heart would ever heal.

"Mandy? You okay?" Emily called.

Finally, Mandy brushed the tears away, and walked out for lunch.

She paused in the living room and looked out the large window. Nope. Still no sign of her brother.

Mandy huffed and stomped to the kitchen, grabbed a plate, heaped food on it and sat at the table.

"Mandy, do you...?" Brad's question halted when he saw her chewing and shoveling.

She waited for him to finish, but he started eating and then turned to everyone else for conversation. She figured if her mouth was full, she wouldn't be asked any more questions.

Lunch was quickly over. Mandy asked to go for a walk. Maybe she could find a shelter of some sort for when Yellowstone erupted.

She stepped out into the crisp air and pulled her jacket close. This was miserable. She should've been on the way to safety, not sitting in a house with two children who smelled and drooled. She kicked at a rock and kept walking.

An hour later, exhausted, she'd walked the entire property and saw no sign of her brother or a shelter. On the up side, Charlie followed the whole way, happy to be out. Mandy talked to her as if they were best friends. She wondered how Charlie and other animals would survive the blast. It made her sad. Finally she headed for the house, hoping to fall into a deep, deep, deep sleep.

Mandy entered, and saw Emily and Brad hanging onto every word the anchor said. The news information hadn't changed since she'd gotten there, but she was surprised at how intent they now were. They turned to stare when she walked in, looking her up and down as if they analyzed whether to eat her.

"Have a seat please."

She sat on the edge of the couch, getting ready to bolt if this conversation went south.

"We've been talking. The President has confirmed what the aliens said. They've given people the information on the collection sites. One is in Casper."

"Ah huh," Mandy said.

"I don't think she understands what you're getting at, honey," Brad said.

"Mandy, we want you to take our girls on an alien ship. We need to know someone is there to watch and protect them. I know you're sad now, but I also believe you were sent to us to do this. You'll survive and go on, and . . . you'll care for our little girls."

"I'm not going anywhere, but with my brother."

"You're our only hope. They can't stay here. We know it's not safe this close to Yellowstone," Brad said.

"Besides the aliens won't take us, and we don't have any other family near," Emily added.

Mandy was shocked. There was no way she would board a ship with two children, especially a ship filled with aliens. "Have you considered this could be an alien invasion?" she asked. "They could be getting ready to take all of us and do

204

weird things to our bodies. Look, why don't you save yourselves? Get away from here, drive north."

"There's not enough time," Brad said. "Listen, you don't have a choice. Tomorrow, early we leave for Casper. You'll board that ship with our children. And frankly, I don't care if you want to or not. We're not discussing this further."

Mandy stood and walked into the bedroom, slamming the door behind her. Charlie was right on her heels. So this was how life was going to end, on an alien ship with two kids who were strangers. She grew angrier and angrier. She stomped around the room and then finally settled, on the bed staring at the ceiling. If he didn't show up soon, she was in big trouble. Mandy tossed and turned, but finally fell asleep with images of weird, orange people dancing around her while she bobbed on a skewer, roasting over a fire.

Chapter 32

"Hey."

Johnny felt a shoe nudge him.

"Get up. You guys can't be here."

Johnny squinted to see a tall nurse in scrubs. "You need to get out of here," he repeated. "They kicked out everyone not in a bed last night. They find you, they'll arrest you."

Johnny shook Wesley first, then Trisha.

"I said, you need to get out of here," the nurse shouted.

They rose to their feet groggily. "We didn't know. We needed a place to . . ."

"Didn't you hear me? Get out! Or I'll call hospital security."

"Where should we go?"

"Don't know. Don't care. Not here." The nurse followed them down the now-deserted hallways and watched as they stepped outside into the cold.

Trisha pulled her sweater closer around her shoulders. "He wasn't very nice at all," she said. "You'd think what with the world ending and all, people would be more considerate."

"Now what?" Wesley asked.

Johnny looked both ways. Empty cars lined the street. There wasn't a soul in sight. The sky held a pinkish hue. "What time is it anyway?" Johnny asked. Looking at his watch, he added. "Seven."

"Does anyone know someone from Casper?"

"Sure, just not anyone's last name or telephone number," Wesley replied.

"We should go to the high school. I'm sure kids are still there. Some of the teams," Johnny said.

"Isn't that, like miles from here?" Trisha asked.

"Yep," Wesley said.

"Which is why we should start walking now," Johnny added and led them down the street.

Trisha hesitated once they reached the end of the block. "I don't think I can make it," she said. She pointed to her high-heeled shoes.

Johnny hadn't given any thought to the fact she'd worn heels. He stared off into the distance. In the morning's half-light, he could see white snow-banks lining the street and sidewalk. "We'll have to help you." Johnny reached for her arm and motioned for Wesley to take her other.

Several times the boys prevented Trisha from slipping and falling. Soon, they had a steady rhythm.

Wesley looked at the sky and pointed out the Eastern Star and Venus both, which were still visible. "Where do you think we'll go?"

They'd decided to leave with the aliens. Johnny shook his head. He'd started to wonder about that himself. There was a part of him second-guessing the decision. "I don't know," he finally admitted. A part of him was a bit excited about the adventure of it all.

"Anyplace will be better than here, if what Gillian said was true." Trisha leaned on Johnny when she stepped on a slick patch of ice.

"What exactly did she tell you?" Wesley asked.

Johnny shrugged. "Yellowstone is unstable. It's a super volcano that's going to erupt. People here don't stand a chance. It's going to throw the world into another ice age," he said the words reluctantly. Each sentence confirmed the choice to go with the aliens was the right one.

The sky above turned from indigo to pastel blue, and in the east, they saw pink. After the first two miles, they pretty much stopped talking, saving their breath for the long walk. At times Trisha had no trouble, but then they'd hit an icy spot and she'd almost take both boys down with her.

"Almost there," Johnny announced when they spotted the high school in the distance.

"Where is everyone?" Wesley asked.

Johnny's head shot up. He searched the empty parking lots.

"Now what?" Trisha asked. Her feet stopped and she jerked both Wesley and Johnny to a standstill.

Johnny's mouth opened and closed. He turned and looked back up the street from where they'd just come. "I. . ." They hadn't seen anyone since they'd left the hospital. Where had everyone gone?

"They all left," Trisha announced. "Not only Mark and the team, but all the teams." She shivered.

"Let's keep going," Johnny finally spoke. "Maybe there are some kids in the school. Maybe the busses are getting gas or something and they'll be back." Johnny really didn't believe what he said, but they'd walked too far and had nowhere else to go.

The sidewalk led to the main entrance. Wesley let go of Trisha's arm and ran the last few yards to open the door. He pulled and pulled. The door was locked.

208

Johnny strode forward and stuck his face against the glass to look in.

"You see anyone?" Trisha asked. She stood beside him, face pressed next to his.

"It's dark. I can't see a thing." Johnny stepped back and saw Wesley walking along the school. "Where are you going?" he asked.

"Maybe the quake broke a window and we can get in," Wesley said and kept walking away.

"That's a good idea. You wait here," Johnny told Trisha. "And I'll go the other way and see if I can find a way in. I'll be back soon."

"No." Trisha's hand snaked out and grabbed Johnny's arm. "Don't leave me alone. I'll go with you."

"Trisha, you can't. Your shoes," he said.

"I don't care. I'm going with you."

Johnny bit his lower lip and stomped off, shaking his head. "I'll be right back to get you."

When he turned the corner he saw Trisha trailing behind. "You're going to get sick, then what?" he demanded.

Trisha ignored him and kept coming, her shoes digging into the snow that drifted against the sides of the school.

Johnny looked beyond her. Wesley had already turned the corner and was no longer in sight. "Come on," he said and he took her arm again.

They were almost at the back of the school when they heard Wesley's excited shout. Johnny released Trisha and ran to the back corner, running into Wesley when they met.

"What?" Johnny asked.

"Someone left a garage door to the shop open," Wesley said.

"That was us," Trisha said as she joined them.

Wesley let Trisha take the lead and Johnny dropped back.

"If you left the shop door open why didn't you think of it?" Wesley asked.

Johnny didn't answer. He wanted to get someplace warm. His feet were freezing and he couldn't imagine what Trisha's felt like.

They entered the shop and quickly pulled the door down, closing out the cold air.

"That wasn't too smart," Trisha announced. They stood in the dark. "Where was the light switch?"

"We didn't have one, remember. The power was out. We used flashlights," Johnny said.

"Okay. Where are the flashlights then?"

Wesley found one on a bench and flipped it on. A weak beam cut through the room. He turned it toward the walls.

"By the door," Johnny instructed.

They found the light switch and one for the hallway too.

Trisha shivered again. "We left some of our stuff. I wonder if it's still here? If so, I have boots!"

Johnny and Wesley followed Trisha through the school and into the atrium.

"Nothing," she said, with hands on her hips. "I can't believe someone would take our stuff."

Johnny slowly turned. He noticed a dark lump and walked towards it cautiously. When he stood over it, he saw it was a blanket. "Is this ours?" he asked.

Trisha dashed to his side. She fell to her knees. "Yeah," she said.

210

They quickly found some warm clothes and extra socks for Trisha, whose toes were numb. Huddled together, it didn't take long for their stomachs to start to rumble.

"Did you guys find any food in this joint?" Wesley asked.

"There are a few vending machines. I wonder if there's anything left," Trisha said, rising from the floor. "Let's go see. I'm starving."

They found a soda machine in the teachers' lounge. "You got any money on you?" Johnny asked Wesley.

Wesley shook his head and then started to shake the machine.

"Docs that work?" Trisha asked. Johnny shrugged.

"I don't know, but it's worth a try isn't it?" Wesley said.

"If not we can always break the glass," Trisha replied.

Johnny walked away. The sun was up and it was easier to see into the closed classrooms. He headed down the hall, peering in the glass doors. A few minutes later, he spied what he was looking for. He pulled out his driver's license and slipped it between the door and jamb. The latch slipped out of the way and the door swung open. "Hey guys," he called.

Trisha stuck her head out of the lounge. "You find something?"

Trisha walked out and Wesley followed.

Inside the classroom, partially hidden behind a screen, stood a small fridge. Johnny opened the door and reached in. It was stacked with sodas and bottles of water. "Jackpot," he said.

"Jackpot would be some food," Trisha announced as she pulled the tab on the soda. She lifted it to her lips and took a long swallow.

Wesley started his and still hadn't stopped drinking. Johnny walked to the desk and opened each drawer, shoving things out of his way. "Bingo!" He threw a protein bar to each of them before taking one for himself.

"You think we're going to get into trouble?" Wesley asked.

Both Trisha and Johnny thought his comment was funny, they grabbed their sides and couldn't stop laughing for several seconds. "The world as we know it is ending. I don't think I care if we get in trouble," Johnny replied.

"Oh, yeah," Wesley said.

Johnny pulled out some candy and a couple of bags of chips. "Breakfast," he announced.

They each took a handful of goodies and returned to the atrium. Finding soft chairs, they sat and quickly devoured the food.

Chapter 33

P.J. woke early the next morning to get on the road. He was far enough from the initial blast area, but felt it was better to keep moving forward. Soon, he hoped, Mandy and Derek would join him. He stopped only when he needed gas and avoided the lines of people and onlookers when he could. The radio kept repeating the same information. The only change, The President wasn't talking like it was a hoax.

P.J. shifted in his seat and wished he had a driving buddy. It would have made the trip go faster. He'd talked to the older couple at the B&B the night before and told them about Yellowstone. They didn't want to leave their home. His mind, in the quiet of the truck, wandered to Sherry. He hated not knowing if she was okay. Then his mom's voice invaded his thoughts, telling him to stay focused on where he was headed.

It was time for a break. He hoped to find a gas station with some decent CD's. Highway signs led him to Lethbridge, where he made a sharp left into a parking lot. It was packed and P.J. was stuck, unable to back out or move forward. So, he stayed, waiting his turn at the pump. This was the first sign to him that things were not normal. Everything to this point had been quiet and serene, almost as if people weren't sure what to believe. P.J., too, thought it all unbelievable. In fact, he wondered, if he hadn't heard Gillian's story, what would he have done?

Finally, it was his turn at the pump; he pulled forward. Around the corner two rambunctious kids charged toward him, hitting each other with swords.

"I got you."

"No, you didn't. I'll kill you, earthling. Come with me or else."

"I don't take orders from orange potato-head men," the other kid shouted.

"Then I'm done with you."

The two children battled again until their mom yelled for them to climb back into the R.V. and to stop hitting each other.

P.J. shook his head, chuckling. He'd always played cowboys and Indians, not cowboys and aliens. He walked inside. The line stood still and two older gentlemen in front of him discussed the likelihood of the situation. Was it possible? Were the aliens really here to help? Or was this the prank of the century? If they had young children, would they let them go? Of course, the big question was: which was worse, going with aliens or staying behind?

The guys chatted loudly, while other patrons joined in every once in awhile with their opinion. A young mother, three customers back, had tears running down her cheeks. She clutched her two year old and a loaf of bread. The little one cried for a drink, while his mom tried to comfort him.

P.J. stepped out of line, walked to the coolers, grabbed some milk and handed it to the mother.

"No, thank you," she said.

214

"It's okay, take it," P.J. said. He was confused. The mother looked down at her shoes. Her lips moved, but he had no idea what she was saying. "Please take the milk. It'll calm him down."

The mother looked into P.J.'s eyes. "I only have a gold necklace to trade and I need bread. We can live off bread and water for a few days. Milk will feed him for a few minutes."

P.J. stepped back, shocked at this mother's confession. "Necklace?"

The clerk at the counter yelled "next" and P.J. realized it was his turn. He put his stuff on the counter, looked back and saw the mom put the bread back. She couldn't say no to her kid, even at a time like this. P.J. took out his fifty bucks.

"Your money is no good here," the cashier told him.

"What? I need gas." He pulled out a credit card.

"Listen, there's an emergency situation going on. No cash, checks or credit. You got food, bottled water, tires or gold and you can gas up. Otherwise, move on."

"I've got a spare tire," P.J. said. "I need to fill up," he leaned forward, "and I want to pay for that ladies' stuff."

The clerk agreed. P.J. moved toward the door, hiding behind a sunglass rack to make sure the clerk did what he'd asked.

Tears streamed down the mother's face, she hugged her child and asked someone to grab the bread she had put down. She happily received her two items. When she walked out, she had a smile from ear to ear.

P.J. waited a few moments, then slipped out and brought in his spare tire. For the first time, P.J. understood why his parents did what they did. Giving back helped ease the ache others felt.

After that, town after town became a blur in the mirror. At some stations he found they would take his credit cards, others only cash and at one, he traded his blanket. He'd stopped only to take care of business or to stretch his legs for a second. He put gas in the car when it dropped to a half tank. Still, he moved forward, tapping the wheel in tune with a beat in his head.

Finally, after fifteen hours of driving, he had no energy left. He pulled into a rest area, not caring where he was. He locked his doors, climbed into the back seat, bunched up a shirt to use as a pillow, and dreamed of his lost days fighting cowboys and Indians.

March 20th

Chapter 34

Mandy woke with a start. She saw a figure in her room and opened her mouth to scream as the male tumbled over the backpack. He grunted.

"Mandy? Get up. It's me," Derek hissed.

"Heroic, brother."

"I try," Derek whispered.

"Thank God you're finally here. I thought they locked all the doors. How'd you get in?"

"Let's talk about that later. We have to go. Why is this dog staring at us?"

"That's Charlie." Mandy hopped out of bed and quickly grabbed the pair of jeans she'd worn last night. She slipped on her shoes and gave Charlie a pat on the head, grabbed her bag and went to follow her brother out the bedroom door. "Wait," Mandy said. All of a sudden she realized by going with Derek she was leaving the family to find someone else to care for their kids on the spaceship. She suddenly felt kind of guilty.

"What?"

"I have to leave a note. It's not fair. They'll worry. They're really nice people."

"We don't have time. We have to get on the road and get out of town before the sun comes up."

"It's not going to be light for a while." Mandy set her bag down and dug through it for paper and a pen.

I have to leave with my brother.
Sorry I can't help you. I have my own
path to take. I wish you the best of luck.
                                    Mandy

Mandy laid it down on the pillow and then smoothed the blanket. She turned toward the door and slipped out of the room. Derek tiptoed in front of her. She thought they were going out the front door and was getting ready to whisper to him the door squeaked, when he walked through the living room and into the kitchen. Mandy sensed Charlie behind her. She wanted to tell the dog to stay, but was afraid to speak. They'd have to part ways at the door. She was sad to leave Charlie behind. She was never a dog person before, but in a short time, Charlie had become her friend.

Derek opened a side door off the kitchen, and they stepped out into the cool breeze of the night. Charlie pushed her way out before Mandy could turn and close the door. "Inside," Mandy whispered to Charlie. She pointed to the door as Emily had done earlier in the day. The dog barked.

"Shut it up or someone's going to hear," Derek hissed.

"Too late," Mandy whispered and pointed to an upstairs window where a light now shone.

"Run!" Derek whispered and sprinted to a patch of trees at the side of the house.

Mandy slowly shut the door, hoping the person didn't hear. She ran to the trees where her brother hid. She and

220

Charlie joined Derek in time to see the front porch door swing open.

They held their breath. Mandy thought for sure the dog knew they were hiding. Charlie was stiff and quiet as well. They were lucky. Most of the spring snow had melted so they hadn't left footprints.

Whoever was on the porch looked around for a moment, then went back inside. The trio waited a few more minutes. When they were ready to stand, the side door opened and someone stepped outside to look around again. This time, seeing no one, they shut the door quickly. A minute later, Mandy and Derek saw another light upstairs go on.

"Derek, we can't leave her," Mandy said pointing to Charlie.

"I know, let's go. The truck is this way. We don't dare go on the main road now."

Mandy looked at Charlie. She figured eventually the dog would go back home, but right now she seemed content to move forward. Charlie nudged her hand and Mandy obediently caressed her large head.

After several minutes, Mandy scanned the surrounding trees. She was grateful for the moon, which beamed brightly in the sky.

"Where's the truck? I thought you said you were parked close by?"

"Yeah, but I'm taking the scenic route."

Mandy laughed. "So, we're lost? We should've stayed on the road? It's the middle of the night. No one would be out."

"Not a good idea. There might be traffic with everything going on, and with a big white dog, we're more noticeable.

We don't want neighbors recognizing her." Derek picked a twig off the ground and stuck it in his mouth.

"So we're not lost?"

"No, the truck is right up here."

Mandy didn't know how her brother could tell where he was, but she believed him. He had the same sense of direction as their father. Together, the two of them saved many lives. When a hiker or skier would turn up missing, her father and brother were always a part of the search and rescue team. They were two of the best trackers in the state. Her father said he always had a gut feeling. Derek called it luck. Together they were almost never wrong.

Mandy tripped over a log. She screamed in pain when a branch cut into her arm.

"You all right?"

"Yes." Drops of blood began to color the scattered snow beneath her feet.

"Try to stop the bleeding. Hold your shirt against it tight. That way blood doesn't drip everywhere."

Derek kicked at the snow. "Doubt anyone will walk this way."

They continued. Mandy held her shirt to her arm. When she finally thought she couldn't go farther, they walked out of the trees. The truck gleamed in shiny happiness in front of her.

Mandy opened the passenger door, and signaled for Charlie to jump in. She placed her few belongings on the floor of the truck and settled in, exhausted and wanting nothing more than to close her eyes and sleep.

"You can sleep later," Derek said roughly. "Clean your arm with this and wrap it."

222

Derek took his duffel bag from behind the seat. He pulled out some junk food and bottles of water and offered them to her.

"How long did it take us to walk here?" Mandy asked.

"Thirty minutes."

"It felt longer. By the way how did you find me?"

"Nothing in a small town is a secret. I asked around."

Derek climbed in and fastened the seat belt. Turning on the engine, he handed a map to Mandy.

"Take a look and tell me which direction I'm heading when I get to Riverton."

Mandy unfolded the map. Her brother had outlined the roads to Oracle, Arizona. The path would keep them on secluded back roads until they got out of the small po-dunk towns in Wyoming. Mandy realized her brother didn't want to tempt fate and get stopped.

"I thought we were going to go to Alaska?"

"Too late now. We're going south. To the Biosphere."

"Okay. We have to head south towards Rawlins, then you're good for a while," Mandy instructed.

"We'll pull over before the sun comes up, but after that, minimal stops only. We have nineteen hours ahead of us and we don't want to waste time."

"Derek?"

"Yes."

"Thank you." Mandy was quiet for a moment. "They wanted me to go with the aliens. Wanted me to take their kids."

"They what?"

Mandy closed her eyes ignoring her brother's question. "Do you think the others are safe?"

223

"I don't know. P.J. should be pretty far if he stuck to the plan."

"I wish we could join him."

"I know Mandy, but we're out of time. That little detour took us a day. I'm sure everyone is fine."

"Think we'll see them again?"

"Honestly?"

Mandy nodded.

"No, kid; we're on our own now."

"Too bad. I really liked them all." She closed her eyes. Mandy was determined to stop wishing for the impossible.

Her dreams took her flying. She soared above the land, like a bird, watching as the ground lifted and shifted, as Yellowstone erupted and spewed it's noxious contents into the air. She dived and tried to divert, but found there was too much stuff.

The truck bumped around the road, and woke her.

"Good morning," Derek greeted her.

"Where are we?"

"Outside of Dove Creek. It's almost eleven."

"I slept a long time. Can we stop? I need to go to the bathroom, and I'm sure Charlie does too."

"No, she's good. We stopped a few miles back. But there's a gas station at the next exit. You missed a beautiful sunrise."

Mandy thought Derek was teasing her. She'd never known her brother to pay attention to anything around him.

"Oh, yeah."

"Yeah, I woke up in time to see it."

"Wake-up? When did you sleep?"

"About three-thirty. I pulled over and closed my eyes for a little while."

"Why didn't you wake me? I could've driven."

"I tried. You rolled towards the door and started snoring."

"Sorry. Do you need more sleep? I'm up now."

"I'll let you start driving after we stop. Don't know if I'll sleep, but it would be nice to get a break. How's the arm?"

She looked at the bandage around her forearm. "It's okay. A little sore."

Mandy stared out the window at the passing shrubbery. She didn't want to tell her brother it might be infected. She'd wait and see if the situation changed. If it didn't, she'd tell him.

They kept going until out the window, she saw nothing but dirt.

No green trees, no pretty flowers blooming. In Arizona, there was just ugly brown dirt. Mandy listened to the radio and the now familiar story: The President will be updating you soon, earthquakes around the world, blah, blah, blah.

"Have you been listening to this all night?"

"Yes, and there's nothing new being reported. A lot of rumors and even those are dumb."

"How come places are still open and people aren't flooding the roads? It's so quiet."

"Some think it's a stupid hoax. I'm sure others are in place for pick-up. But there are a few who probably hope if they ignore it, all will go away and things will be normal again.

"What do you wish for, Derek?"

"For us to arrive safely. You?"

"I wish Mom and Dad were here."

Derek didn't respond. Instead he stared straight ahead. He pulled into a gas station on the edge of a small town and narrowly missed a pole.

"Geez, Derek."

"Sorry, I was thinking."

"Well, think when the truck is shut off and you can't kill us."

They pulled next to the pumps; Derek hopped out and began pumping gas. Mandy headed inside to take care of business. She hadn't realized how hungry she was.

"Derek, you want food?" she called over her shoulder.

"Yeah, meet you at the counter."

"Can we grab something for Charlie? She probably needs water."

"Way ahead of you." Derek pulled out a used serving bowl from behind the seat and showed it to her.

"You old softy."

"Mom must have left it in there after the last church potluck."

Mandy's eyes watered. She forced a smile, turned on her heel and walked into the store. A little bell chimed above the door when she entered. A young guy about her age sat behind the counter, his feet propped up, arms behind his head and muscles flexed.

"Hey," he said.

"Hey. You know the world's ending? Why are you still here and open?"

"No place else to go to see the fireworks. Plus when it gets real bad, I plan to shut off the cooler and eat junk food until it's over. See, I have all the supplies I'll need. Chips,

226

soda, water, bread and peanut butter, oh, and I have this." He picked up a duffel bag that lay at his feet. Mandy didn't think it could hold much. What would help a person survive this type of disaster she wanted to ask, but didn't want to pee in his Wheaties.

"Well then, glad to hear you're prepared."

"I'm Jesse." He stuck out his hand.

Mandy grabbed it and shook, feeling awkward. "Mandy. My brother's name is Derek. He's pumping gas."

"Well, help yourself to whatever you want," he said.

Mandy moved away from the counter and headed towards the restrooms at the back of the store. She wanted to believe he'd be okay. She shook her head, not wanting to start crying in a strange, smelly bathroom. By the time she came out, her brother was at the counter, and Jesse was showing him the duffle. Mandy smiled, despite herself. Jesse was so animated and cute. Someone she would've been awkward around a few days before.

"Mandy, he says we can load up the truck. There's plenty here for all of us. I'll get it organized in here. You go get the truck."

"Won't your boss be mad when he finds out you gave a bunch of his merchandise away?"

"I don't know. I don't exactly work here. But I'm pretty sure the cameras don't work."

"How do you know?"

"I broke them when I wandered in. The door was unlocked. I think the place was abandoned, but you never know."

"Why are you staying here then, posing like you work here?"

"I already told you. They have a reinforced freezer and Twinkies, and if I'm not here, someone else would be."

Mandy shook her head. It didn't make sense to her, but he seemed convinced this was a great plan.

When she walked out and climbed in the truck, Charlie greeted her with a wet, sloppy kiss. Mandy scratched behind the dog's ears, put the truck in reverse and backed up to the sidewalk. She secretly hoped Derek remembered her favorite cookies were Nutterbutters and Butterfingers, her favorite candy. Immediately, she was plagued with a feeling of guilt. They were thieves. They shouldn't take someone else's stuff. Mandy told her conscience they had to do it and made a promise, if they survived, she would pay back every dime.

She put the truck in park and let Charlie wander while Derek loaded the goods. Derek and Jesse came out with box after box. Cereal, bread, peanut butter, noodles, protein bars, dog food, cases of water and juice. Mandy went inside to see if anything was left on the shelves. She found an old radio, a pair of pink rhinestone sunglasses and a dog collar to match. She picked up the sunglasses and tried them on. Looking for a mirror, she felt someone behind her. She quickly took them off.

"They look good on you," Jesse said. "Here's a leash. It may come in handy, too."

"Thank you. This was really nice of you."

"Good luck, come back and see us real soon. I mean if the world doesn't end and all, and you're passing through."

Mandy smiled. She leaned forward and kissed him on the cheek. "Be safe," she said, as heat crept up her cheeks.

Derek looked at her when she hopped into the driver's seat. "You all right?"

228

"Yeah, fine." Mandy put the truck in drive and looked in the rearview mirror. The boy stood on the porch staring at her.

"He wouldn't come with us," Derek said.

"What?"

"Jesse. I asked him if he wanted to join us, he said no."

Jesse slipped inside the store.

"Oh well, I hope he makes it then."

"Me, too." Derek pulled out a traveling pillow and blanket. Charlie laid her head on Derek's lap and stretched across the seat kicking Mandy. Mandy scooted closer to the door to give the dog more room.

She looked back one last time to see Jesse jogging toward them his duffle slung over one shoulder. Mandy hit the brakes and rolled down the window.

"Maybe you're right. I've always wanted to see the Grand Canyon. I'll jump in the back."

Derek nodded. Mandy rolled up the window, smiled and drove forward. Charlie sighed and fell into a deep, loud-snoring sleep.

Mandy opened a soda and sipped while she wondered what they would find in Oracle, Arizona. The radio station interrupted her thoughts with the same information played twenty minutes ago. It listed pick-up sites, told people not to panic and said the White House had been dark since The President's second speech. Mandy wished for some good country music to interrupt the all-important broadcast and give her a distraction. Or perhaps she could trade the sleeping Derek with Jesse.

Deciding it was more important for Derek to sleep, she reached under the seat hoping to find tapes stashed there. Right now she was grateful for the little things in life she

229

could count on staying the same. Mandy opened the case, found what she was looking for and placed it into the player. Shania Twain's, "*I Feel Like a Women*," filled the cab.

Mandy, Derek, and Jesse drove for several long, boring hours, taking turns. At times Mandy tried to strike up a conversation about their parents or friends back home, but mostly they sat in silence, grunting a response or two back and forth.

At one point, around Globe, Mandy fell asleep and dreamed of being a little girl. She was hiking in Wyoming. Her parents and her brother were there. Flowers covered the base of the mountain, pretty yellow and purple ones. Mandy wanted to pick them all and take them home. Her dad came up behind her.

"Mandy, the mountain likes its flowers. Leave them."

She giggled, "I know Daddy, but I want to take them home." Mandy's dad reached for her hand. "Come on, buttercup, let's start walking."

She put down the flowers and walked beside her dad. He was so tall. She had to strain to look up at him. Mandy felt warm. Soon they started to walk uphill and her dad let go of her hand. She kept climbing and looking up, but her dad wasn't there anymore. Her mom came up behind her.

"Come on, sweetheart. Keep up."

Mandy's mom passed her and Mandy tried to walk faster. "Mommy, your legs are longer. Wait up."

Her mother stopped and turned toward her, "You can do it. I'll wait right here for you. Keep climbing."

Mandy walked a little way, but the higher she climbed the farther away her mom seemed to be. She gripped the side of the mountain with both hands and climbed. She started to slip on loose gravel.

"Mandy, you can do it," her mom told her from above.

"Please, Mommy, pull me up."

"No, you can do this on your own."

Her hands slipped and tears streamed down her face, wetting the front of her shirt.

"Mommy, please, you have to help me. I can't do it without you."

"Believe," her mom told her. "You'll be fine."

Suddenly Derek's face replaced her mother's, and he pulled her up to a ledge. Mandy clung to him, sobbing. Her mother left when she needed her most.

Mandy startled awake.

"You okay?" Derek asked, staring at her oddly.

"Fine, why?"

"You were dreaming."

"How do you know I was dreaming?"

Derek gave her a look. "Because I'm your brother and I know."

"Oh."

Mandy turned toward the window. Did the dream mean her mom believed she could do anything she wanted? Or that she needed Derek to save her? She crossed her arms over her chest and slunk down. How could her mom not save her?

Derek turned on the radio and opened the sliding back window. Jesse stuck his head in.

"You doing okay?"

"Yeah. A bit windy is all.

A talk show announcer discussed the evacuation spots.

Then they cut to a woman with a high-pitched voice, at one of the sites. "It's like a circus here," the caller said. "There are booths everywhere. We witnessed someone being saved, and right beside them you can buy cotton candy. The ships are hovering above, and people are lined up and waiting. We haven't gotten a glimpse of the aliens yet."

"Okay, thanks for calling in. Listeners, we'll have more details for you as things develop. Next, we're going to talk to a scientist who has done research on Yellowstone's caldera. Welcome, Dr. Desmond."

"Thank you for having me."

"I'm sure the listeners want to know, how are things at Yellowstone?"

"We're feeling tiny earthquakes. The area has become unstable and the caldera is rising. We've also noticed new splits. The animals have evacuated and so should you."

"How long do people have to leave the area?"

"We don't know for sure. It could be an hour. It could be a day. What I would say is you need to leave now and drive as far, as fast, as you can. We don't want panic and chaos. But this is going to happen."

Mandy shut off the radio. "I don't want to know."

"Me either," Jesse added.

Chapter 35

P.J. woke as sun streamed in his window and car horns blared around him. He sat up only to see the parking lot was blocked, people and cars were everywhere. He climbed out to ask what was going on. A couple walked by hand in hand as though out for an afternoon stroll, not in the middle of a sea of people.

"What's happening?" P.J. asked.

"It's Collection Day," the young women answered. "That's Calgary. It's a pick-up zone."

There was no way he could move his car. P.J. grabbed his backpack and a water bottle, then headed up the road on foot. He might as well watch the entertainment. He would stay until it was over. Then come back, get his car and head to Alaska. He passed people, memories and hope tucked into small bags clasped under tiny arms.

He kept close to the side of the road, trying to avoid the circus of people. There were open fields and people hung out to watch the spectacle. There were vendors selling t-shirts, toys, candy, soda and water. He shook his head. Why did some people use every opportunity to make a buck? Some people walked around with signs warning others to not send their children. P.J. really wished he had a headset so he could drown out the noise.

He wasn't sure what he would do. If he had children, would he send them? Would he keep them close and hope to protect them himself? Would it work to ride out the storm close to home? He had no idea, and a part of him was glad he wasn't in that situation. He wouldn't know what it was like to say goodbye to a child you loved, hoping you weren't condemning them to a life of hell and unhappiness. The world was changing, no doubt, and whatever decision you made, somehow you lost.

He walked, trying to block out the feelings that welled up inside him. The crowd stopped moving and he was forced to stand with them. He jumped up to see over the people's heads, hoping to discover the cause. Two young boys caught his attention.

They seemed to be alone, but with so many people, P.J. wasn't sure. Their parents could have been standing two feet away and he wouldn't know it. The older brother, who was about ten, was trying hopelessly to calm his younger brother. P.J. shifted again, trying to decide if he should intervene.

"Excuse me," P.J. said, finally deciding. "Is everything okay?"

"I want my mom," replied the younger child.

His older brother kicked him in the shin and, with teeth clenched, told his brother to shut-up.

"No, I want Mom. We can't leave. Mom told us to wait here for her. She wants to say good-bye before we get on the ship."

"You and your brother have been on the side of the road for how long?"

"Hours. But now the ship is here. We have to go. This is what Mom wants," relayed the older child.

234

P.J. looked around. She was probably lost in the thick of the crowd and unable to find them. How scary for her. She would always wonder if her boys actually made it.

"We have to get on that ship," the older boy said. A gold-colored ship with a few lights on the outside hovered above the ground. P.J. shook his head in disbelief. As he'd been walking he'd thought it was some sort of tent, now that he was closer he could truly see it. Just like in the movies. A flying saucer with lights that sparkled on and off. Holy cow!

"Yeah, cool, huh?" the older boy said.

"Mom says it's going to save us, and we should wait right here while she gets information about all of this. She wouldn't let us leave without saying good-bye, I know she'll find us," the younger boy argued.

"Okay," P.J. said. "How about you stay with me until she returns or it's time for you to board the ship. Ouch!" P.J. turned. A big, balding man with a "Repent Before Evil Comes" sign stepped on his heel.

"Anything you need forgiveness for?" the man asked.

"No." P.J. turned around. "Boys let's move out of the way of the nice man." He steered them away from the religious people and the baptism going on in the field behind them.

"Let's move closer to the ship. That way you'll be ready to board when it's time. Do you have a picture of your mom?"

"Why?" the younger one asked.

"Well, if you have a picture, I can search the crowd for her while we wait. And in the event we don't find her in time, I'll keep looking. Then I can tell her you guys are safe."

The little one took out a wrinkled picture from his back pocket. It showed the three of them and half of someone else's arm. The boy tried to smooth it out on his pants. "Here, you can look at it, but you can't keep it. I've had it a long time."

P.J. took a quick look and handed it back to the little boy, his hand shook a little.

"I'm Mack. This is Lee."

"Nice to meet you both. I'm P.J."

They each held onto one of P.J's hands as they moved into the line to get onto the ships. He wasn't sure what time they would start moving kids on, but he hoped it was soon. He didn't really want to hang around longer than necessary. The energy around him was weird and it was giving P.J. the creeps. He noticed the families surrounding him. Some prayed, while others sang and danced to songs of hope and peace. Many clung to their children and cried. P.J. held the boys' hands a little tighter.

The doors to the ship opened and two creatures stepped out. Both were smaller and almost child-sized themselves, but with greenish-blond hair, round faces and longer than normal limbs. It gave them an almost comedic appearance. A ramp lowered to a loading dock where people lined up. Immediately everyone was moved into two different lines. Girls in one and boys in the other.

A tiny wand was held to each child's body by an alien. Then they would point to the next person. Once past the aliens, the kids floated on a walkway into the ship. You couldn't see past the doors, but P.J. was curious enough to try.

Ahead of him, a mom gripped her children tightly until she could go no farther. The beings took her children and moved her out of the way. She screamed and tried to push back, but couldn't get through as though an invisible force

236

kept her back. The children moved across the conveyer belt and disappeared inside.

P.J. faced forward, not sure if he wanted to pull these kids out of line and take them. He waited for his parent's voices to tell him what to do, but his inner thoughts were quiet. The people behind pushed him forward, but he held his ground.

He and the boys stood closer to the dock now and could see the aliens' faces. They were emotionless, doing a job. He believed they could as easily be counting sheep. He didn't get a warm, fuzzy feeling and it worried him. He might be handing these young boys into an unsafe situation. On the other hand, these weren't his children to make a decision for. If they were, they'd have been in the car and on their way to a safe place, not boarding the spaceship with aliens. Indecisive at first, it was clear to him now.

Twenty minutes later and P.J. had only moved inches closer. The aliens nodded to each other, turned around, and walked onto the spacecraft. The doors closed and the ship rose. P.J. wasn't sure what was going on. Were they done? Were they coming back? He wished the aliens would at least communicate effectively.

P.J. saw the confused faces around him; he stood still, not sure what to do. He felt a tugging on his sleeve.

"Don't we get to go?" Mack asked. "Don't they want us?"

P.J. shook his head, "I'm not sure what's going on, but I don't think they left because of anything you did. I'm sure they have to drop some people off or send another ship. They'll be back. We'll wait right here. Don't worry."

He felt a growing frustration. P.J. was sure he heard somewhere all healthy children who wanted to go would be allowed to board the ships. He wasn't, of course, sure about the logistics of such a mission, but he wanted to believe he hadn't just become the guardian of two young boys. He was barely taking care of himself at the moment.

"Your boys?"

"What?" P.J. turned to see a man behind him.

"Are those your boys?"

P.J. laughed. "I'm only eighteen. Just helping out."

"That's nice of you."

"Are you going on the ship?"

"I'm going to try. They said the cut off was twenty-three. I just turned twenty-four, but I've been told I look younger."

P.J. didn't think so. "I believe they have ways to detect your age. I've been watching them. They have a special wand. They move people out of the way when they're not what they're looking for."

"Do you really think a few months will make a difference?"

P.J. shrugged and turned away.

"Why don't you let me hold one of the boys' hands?"

"What?" P.J. questioned.

"Yeah. I'll tell the aliens I'm all the little guy has. Inform them I promised my great aunt I'd take care of him."

"I don't think they're into communicating with us."

"How do you know it wouldn't work? What do you know anyway?" The man's voice rose. Lee started to cry. "Are we in trouble?"

P.J. looked at the little boy. He was exasperated that they stood in a ridiculously long line, with nowhere to sit and no water. P.J. didn't even want to be there.

He spun around. "Look, I can see you're desperate, but I'm not going to let you borrow one of these children for your own benefit. I'm helping. If you get on, great. I wish you the best of luck. But if you don't, you can argue with me later, when I don't have the boys with me. Right now, I'm not discussing this with you."

P.J. knelt to look the littlest boy, Mack, in the eyes. "I'm not sure how all of this works. I know I'm older and supposed to be, um, smarter here, but I've never encountered something like this before. What I do know is if those aliens don't take you, it'd be their loss and my gain."

"Why your gain?"

"Well, because I've always wanted two younger brothers to hang out with." P.J. ruffled Mack's hair.

The corners of Mack's mouth turned up as he smiled at P.J.

"You don't have any brothers?" Lee stared at P.J. with inquisitive eyes.

"I do now." P.J. stood and waited for the ship's return.

Within minutes a new ship hovered above the loading dock.

"See, I told you they'd come back for you." P.J. squeezed Lee's hand.

The line moved quickly once the ship began to hover in place. New beings, different looking from the last ones, stood on the plank – short, hairless blue creatures, with long fingers and heart-shaped faces. P.J. didn't notice a wand, but he saw people being moved off to the side if they were not chosen.

He looked at the boys. They were about thirty people from the front.

"Okay, I'm going to leave you here. I can't go any farther."

Mack's eyes pleaded with him not to let go.

"I'll wait right here, off to the side, and watch you board. I promise. I'll find your mom and tell her you made it."

In the middle of P.J.'s speech, a fight broke out ahead and children started pushing and shoving.

"I'm going on. You can't stop me," someone shouted.

"No, you can't. They pointed for you to get out of the way. Now get out of the way and let others board."

"I'm going."

"No, you're not."

One guy took a swing at another. P.J. tried to squeeze the boys closer to him.

"You can't go. They won't let you," someone yelled.

"They said everyone under twenty-three who wanted to, could go. Calm down," someone behind P.J. shouted.

"Stop," someone else from the crowd yelled. "You're hurting my child."

P.J. spotted several young children by themselves. Frightened eyes stared at the adults around them. Things were unraveling quickly. P.J. reached down and picked up Mack, placing a protective arm around Lee. He would do his best to keep them from being knocked down and trampled should the crowd head in their direction. This was worse than a rock concert he'd attended.

He remembered the event all too well. They were crowded into a very small area waiting for something big to happen. As soon as the band came on stage and started

240

playing, the crowd pushed forward to get closer. Several people in the front had to be pulled over the barrier in order to avoid being crushed. And when the crowd didn't stop after the band asked, the band walked off stage, creating chaos in the arena. Finally, he had been lucky enough to find an exit.

Someone stepped on P.J.'s foot and the memory evaporated. As much as he wanted a door to appear to let him get air, there would be none. People pushed in all directions and P.J. felt his grip on Lee loosening. Lee looked up panicked.

"Hold my sleeve. Whatever you do, don't let go," P.J. yelled to be heard above the crowd.

Lee nodded and P.J. felt his little hand grab tighter to the fabric of his sleeve while P.J. moved to create a wider base. He slipped his arm around the boy and held him close to his chest. So, they wouldn't get shoved down. He turned to move the boys down the ramp to leave, pushing against the crowd this time. P.J. couldn't wait for a magic opening; he wanted to take the boys to safety. He was letting his emotions take over. This is crazy, he thought. Someone is going to get seriously injured in here. As he turned to leave with the boys, he heard a little voice from below pleading with the men to stop.

"You're selfish. Move out of the way and let us go," a teenager said to the men who had started the trouble. "If this was any other situation, I could have you arrested for assaulting a kid."

"I'm getting on this ship and you can't stop me."

P.J. grabbed the arm of the older man who swung widely.

"Sir, it's difficult. I realize this. However, we didn't make the decision. They did." P.J. started to set Mack down.

The man turned on P.J. and landed a right hook square to his jaw. This is what happens to nice guys, P.J. thought. Tears appeared in the corners of his eyes.

P.J. shifted Mack to his other arm and let go of Lee. He was tired of being nice and polite. He brought his fist back and was getting ready to hit the guy, when he heard Lee's voice, barely above a whisper.

"Please don't. My dad used to hit."

"Please," Mack pleaded, "If we don't go, we'll die."

P.J. looked down at Lee, who sat on the ground beside him. He unclenched his fist, knelt down and grabbed Mack, feeling disappointment welling up in his chest. How could he be so selfish? Mack could've been trampled; he wasn't fit to be a guardian of anyone.

"I'm sorry. I'm so sorry." He hugged Mack and Lee.

The man moved away from P.J., but the energy in the air was still heated. He was afraid at any moment it could erupt again. It was getting scarier and scarier. He regretted his decision to follow in his parent's footsteps and help out. He could've ignored the children, and kept walking. Hole up in a room somewhere for a few nights and wait it out. Then he'd be in his car, not in the middle of crazy land.

Mack's hand pulled on P.J.'s sleeve, getting his attention. When P.J. looked down Mack was pointing to something.

"Mom!" Lee screamed.

Mack pointed to a woman with tears streaming down her cheeks. She nodded yes. But Lee tried to push out of his arms while Mack pulled, trying to get through the crowd and off the loading area. The crowd held them both in place. P.J. searched the woman's eyes for an answer. He was still waiting when he felt something below his feet begin to move. His feet

242

moved forward but he wasn't taking steps. A long, clear plastic, conveyor belt had come from the ship and slid underneath his feet. He had no idea what was going on, but people were moving in all directions. Some went in the ships, while others were dropped off to one side. A group of young adults tried to run beside the belt with children in tow.

P.J. searched the mother's eyes, needing to know how she felt. Her head nodded "yes," but behind her eyes, there was something more. P.J. grabbed the boys and tried to run off the conveyor belt. Too late. He couldn't leave. They seemed to gain speed as they got closer to the ship's doors.

He held the boys' hands tighter as they were deposited in a shiny white room. The glare from the walls caused him to blink repeatedly.

"Ouch," Mack said.

"Sorry."

P.J. tried to calm his thudding heart. He never wanted this. Instead he was pushed into a ship with two boys he didn't know. And now he was in charge of keeping them safe. His hands began to sweat.

Lee giggled. "You nervous?" he asked.

"A little. You?"

Lee nodded, sadness in his eyes. "I miss Mom already. And I'm hungry."

"I'll see what I can do about food shortly. Right now we have to hang in there."

P.J. felt overwhelmed. He didn't get to say good-bye to anyone. No one would ever know what happened to him. His parents wouldn't know he was safe, wouldn't realize he followed in their footsteps. He'd probably never see Sherry again. He'd never know if his friends, Mandy and Derek,

243

made it to Alaska and were waiting at the prearranged spot for him. He wondered what they'd do when he didn't show.

P.J. found a small space on a wall not already taken by someone. He slid down it, clutching the boys to his side. Nope, this was his life now. He was a guardian of two boys who, in the upcoming years, would need him. The weight of his actions sat heavy on his chest, and thoughts of failure resonated in his brain. Unconsciously, he drummed a beat on his thighs.

Chapter 36

"I think that looks much better," Johnny said.

"I don't think it's going to work," Trisha said.

"Just keep going," Johnny told her. "It looks much better already."

"I look like a freak," Wesley said. He turned toward the bathroom mirror.

It was Collection Day and, when they woke, Wesley's face had an eerie green tinge to it. The wound was healing nicely, but the area around it and the rest of his face was bruised.

Trisha offered Wesley her makeup as a joke. She said she was used to sharing. "My sisters always borrowed my shoes, clothes and make-up. I have some powder, cover-up and two eye shadows." A tear slid down her cheek. "I'm never going to see them again."

Johnny quickly changed the subject. "This is a great idea." He took the eye shadow from Trisha. Johnny huddled in the bathroom trying to cover the shades of purple and black on Wesley's face.

"They're going to notice this," Wesley whined.

"They won't," Johnny insisted.

Earlier they found the computer lab. They'd watched footage as the visitors loaded young people from the East Coast into their ships.

"Some of them look like aliens in the movies and on T.V.," Trisha said.

"Yeah, I know. It makes you wonder, doesn't it?" Wesley added.

When Johnny looked outside, he could see the first of the ships in the distance.

"We should go," Johnny said. He studied the finished product. If someone looked closely, they'd wonder what Wesley was up to, but Johnny hoped the aliens wouldn't be interested.

Trisha gently climbed down from the sink where she'd been perched. "Okay, I'm ready. Let's do this."

The creature said all things would be provided for evacuees and to take nothing but what they wore. Trisha found that difficult. She grabbed a small notebook and pen and stuffed it into her coat. Johnny also rummaged through his stuff and found a photo he wanted to keep. Wesley waited with his hands in his pockets.

"You aren't going to bring anything with you?" Trisha asked.

Wesley shook his head. "I've got a funny feeling they won't be taking me at the 1:00 pick up."

Johnny had listened to his negativity the whole morning. Ever since they'd heard not every young person was being accepted. "Don't worry. You're going," Johnny said. He needed Wesley and Trisha. There was no way he'd live on this planet, or another, without them.

They walked to the shop, out the garage and into the back parking lot. The day was sunny and warmer. Ice now formed puddles that wet their feet as they walked.

"What time is it?" Wesley asked.

246

"They'll be getting ready to board soon," Johnny said without really answering.

The closer they came to the hovering ship the more people they saw. Families stood with signs declaring the end of the world. Johnny shook his head. He didn't think the people said anything new. Several groups held signs that judged the aliens as predators. Soon the three found themselves with other teenagers strolling down the center of the street. Police and sheriff officers lined the area and kept protesters back. A couple of times the crowds surged and Johnny got jostled.

Trisha sneezed repeatedly. Her nose had started to run the night before. Johnny dug into his pocket and handed her a tissue.

"Don't do it. Don't be fooled," an old man shouted in Johnny's ear.

They continued.

Soon the movement slowed and they were standing in line. Johnny stood on tiptoes and tried to see over the crowd. "We're still too far away," he told Wesley and Trisha. "I can't see a thing."

At a backward surge, the ship rose. It hung suspended for a brief moment and then drifted off, quickly gathering speed until it was only a small dot on the horizon. Johnny blinked and noticed another ship land. This time when he rose on tiptoes and peered over the people in front, he could see they were almost at the ramp.

He bit his lower lip and looked at Wesley. They had to get him on board. Johnny tried to see how the process worked. It looked as if the young people were separated by sex, boys to the right on the ramp and girls on the left. They formed a line that went straight into the ship while walking past a series of orange creatures in strange white suits.

Johnny was surprised that none of the protesters had tried to stop the process.

Wesley reached over and tugged on his sleeve. "See that?" he asked.

"What?" Johnny asked.

"A force field." Wesley shook his head. "It keeps the rejected out. Look."

Trisha's gaze followed where Wesley pointed. Sure enough, an invisible force kept back the surging crowd of adults.

Wesley stumbled and Trisha quickly caught him. Worried, Johnny looked to see if any of the creatures had seen it, but they all appeared busy.

"We have to split up," Johnny told Trisha. "But I'll see you on board. Don't be afraid."

Trisha's eyes were wide.

"Okay, Wes. Stick close and keep your head down," Johnny advised, noticing the children who seemed to be given less attention.

Johnny stepped onto the ramp and felt a quiver beneath his feet. Just as a force kept back the crowd, another kept them moving forward in single file. Johnny's stomach churned and for a moment he had the urge to turn and run. One of the creatures reached out an appendage and touched Johnny's arm, startling him.

A thought occurred to him, "You will live."

The creature released him and Johnny moved forward and into the ship. He stood in a corridor. The smell of ginger filled his nostrils. He followed the boy in front of him and thought how eerie the silence was. The hallway led to a large room. Johnny turned and was relieved to see Wesley behind him.

Johnny grinned. "See, no problem," he said.

"When that creature grabbed you, I thought we were done for," Wesley said and produced a weak laugh.

"Me, too." Johnny turned around in a circle. "You see Trisha?"

Wesley searched the crowd. "You're kidding. There's more than a thousand kids in here," Wesley said.

Johnny's brows drew together. He saw the girl who had been right in front of Trisha. She had to be in here somewhere.

"Let's go over and stand by the glass. Maybe we can spot her," he suggested before moving off.

Johnny trailed, his head moving back and forth searching. When they reached the glass they turned and scanned the area again. Even more bodies were now pressed together.

"How many of us are they going to fit in here?" Wesley complained.

"Can you see her?" Johnny asked.

Wesley shook his head.

The girl who'd been in front of Trisha in line was all of a sudden pushed out of the crowd and right at Johnny. "Whoa," he said steadying her. "You okay?"

"Yeah, I'm just..." the girl started to cry.

Wesley turned away and looked outside and down at the crowd who waited to board.

"It's going to be okay. I know it's scary, but it will be good," Johnny said and forced a smile.

"You were the boy with Trisha," the girl said.

Johnny nodded.

"Johnny," Wesley said.

Johnny caught the urgency in his voice, but ignored it.

"She . . . they wouldn't let her come," the girl said. "They said she was sick."

"Johnny!" Wesley grabbed his arm.

Johnny shook him off. "Who?" he asked.

"Trisha!" Wesley yelled and slapped his hand against the glass.

Johnny looked outside. Trisha stood outside the bubble. Her face red and eyes filled with tears.

"No!" Johnny yelled. He pushed his way through the crowd, needing to get to the door.

"Johnny, what are you going to do?" Wesley grabbed his arm and tried to hold him back.

"If Trisha can't go, well then, I'm going to stay too."

"What? Johnny, you don't want to do that." Wesley tugged again and Johnny swung his arm, almost hitting a little girl in the eye.

"Sorry," Johnny mumbled. He continued forward.

The wave of children crushed him and made it almost impossible for him to get anywhere. Across the large room the big doors begin to close.

"No! Wait!" He pushed even harder.

Beside him, Wesley, made room by holding kids back. They were almost to the door when Johnny stumbled over a small child. And when Wesley helped him to his feet, the doors were closed. Above their heads, the dome of the ship lit up and different colored lights flashed.

Johnny lurched toward the door where he pounded and screamed, "Help! Let me out!"

The children, their attention fixed on the ceiling, began to calm. And then on the screen the colors faded and the creature from the television came on.

"Do not become concerned, Water Beings. We are about to leave your planetary zone and will be joining our larger ship. Remain at peace."

Johnny banged on the door one more time. "Please. Let me out."

The ship shuddered. Johnny lost his balance and reached for Wesley's arm. The floor dipped away and the crowd of children worked hard to keep on their feet. Then suddenly, the ship was righted. It rose and Johnny had the feeling he was riding in an elevator. When the sky became black, a shudder tore through the ship and they changed course to move sideways.

"What is going on?" Wesley asked no one in particular. He held onto a young girl of about seven to keep her from falling.

"I feel sick," the little girl said.

"It's going to be okay," Wesley assured her.

"No, I'm going to . . ." She turned away from Wesley and vomited on Johnny's shoes.

Chapter 37

∞

Rohongra waited. Below was a sea of waving life forms. She'd been managing the collection of Hu-Mans, as they called themselves, from her planetary mover, but after hours of watching the smaller transportation discs leave and return, she wanted to see some of the planet.

Before her own life form had matured, her father visited this planetary system. He thought often of the things he saw when she was not fully evolved. Now looking down from the ship at the lovely colors and the moving, shimmery planet, she felt saddened by its death.

Her head moved to see more of the young beings threading their way through the crowds to enter the ship. Rohongra sighed. Dahi was elated the plan worked so well. The Water Planet beings voluntarily came into their ships, happy to be removed from their home.

It helped, no doubt, that Ka initiated the earth movements. And it appeared once started, the earth movements were continuing on their own. Based upon the information her Co-Beings relayed, this particular area also sustained much land shaking. So much so that large water patterns surged up over the embankments to capture unwilling beings, dragging them into the water. She'd felt the loss of their life force.

Rohongra still worried over the decision of the council. They had to know the thoughts of Ka, and of Dahi, through her. How could they allow the removal to happen this way?

∞ -It's time, -∞ Novo, the being in charge of the ship thought.

∞ -Very well.-∞ Rohongra drifted over to view the entities below. She felt so free without her sheath on. If only she could leave ThAak-Too. Many had been collected at this site. The un-mature ones cried against the more mature beings. Rohongra felt weakened. The sadness was invading her Being and causing her agony. There was room for more of the beings. She could order the ship to move on to the next collection site to wait, but she had seen enough.

∞-Let us return,- ∞

Already she felt Dahi's thoughts surge. He was hungry for the beings and what they could deliver to him. Disposables, that is what Dahi considered the Water Planet Hu-Mans. They would be used and discarded. Rohongra glided over to the console that showed the galaxy. So many planets. So many choices for life. She wished she could let them go. Many of the planets would sustain them. She heard Bodha's public thoughts and knew he planned to let the beings he collected go. Rohongra wondered if he'd prepared a planet for them. That information would be worth a lot. Dahi and Ka both would be elated to learn the news. Unprotected Water Planet beings, more disposables that would be available when these ran out. Rohongra knew Bodha would have to be careful.

Chapter 38

Jessica sat at the news desk when the next earthquake hit Los Angeles. As a California native, she'd been through many quakes in her lifetime, but these frightened her. During the last one, she saw the camera lights shake above her, and a chair on rollers whip by. It seemed the jarring movement would never stop. When two large camera lights fell and shattered on the floor, Jessica scuttled under the desk. She didn't care if the camera guys were still filming or not.

And then it was over. Jessica rose from behind her desk, adjusted her skirt and wiped away dust. She nodded to her co-workers and stepped off screen. To the casual observer, it appeared she was going to her dressing room to fix her makeup, which was a good idea since her mascara had smeared and she'd bitten off her lipstick, but she passed the dressing room door and walked outside to the parking lot.

The scene that greeted her was insane. Cars drove by on the side-roads as if this were any other day. Jessica looked out over the studio and toward the area where the spaceship collected evacuees. She couldn't quite see it from where she stood, but knew it had to be close. She checked her watch, then ran to the van that always waited to be sent to the next story.

"Hurry," Jessica told the driver. "We need to get to the collection site as soon as possible."

She arranged herself on the seat beside him. If they hurried, she might be able to make it. She turned her head left and right, trying to see past the large buildings that blocked her view. She knew from the coverage her station had done the area was crowded, but there was still a way for a reporter to get in. She checked her watch again. Twenty more minutes and they would be gone. She had to get to them. "Go faster," she ordered.

"What do you want me to do?" the driver pointed to the cars in front that blocked the way.

"I want you to get to that ship using any means possible," Jessica retorted.

The driver put on his emergency lights and pulled onto the shoulder of the road. They passed car after car. Now they were getting somewhere.

They arrived at the site a few minutes before the final countdown and were waved through by the police who monitored the evacuation.

"Now what?" her driver asked.

"Park. As close as you can." She wondered how fast she could go in her heels. As soon as the van stopped, Jessica was out and running.

"Hey, wait, I need to get the camera . . ." she heard the driver.

But Jessica wouldn't wait. She had to get on board. When word came of the evacuation, Jessica had been somewhat upset. At twenty-six she was considered too old to leave. She wasn't going to have it. She wasn't going to sit by and lose her life.

Jessica elbowed her way through the throngs of people still crowded around the space ship, till she stood in the front of the line. She pulled off her suit coat and kicked off her heels. At the same time, she let her hair down around her shoulders. There, she thought, transformation complete.

She rounded her shoulders. It wouldn't do to appear too confident. Not now. She stepped forward toward the ramp. Stopped by an unknown force, it almost knocked her back. Stunned, she reached out and tried to push. "No!" she screamed. She turned to the crowd behind her. "How do I get in there?" she asked.

"You can't. You're too old," a woman explained.

"But I'm not too old," Jessica whined.

The people looked at her with suspicious eyes.

"There you go, honey. Remember, I love you," a mother made her way forward with her young daughter. She gave her one last hug and guided the girl toward the ramp.

"Wait," Jessica cried. "I'll go with her." She took the girl's hand from the grateful mother. "Let's go, sweetheart," she said.

The girl led and Jessica could see how easily she was able to move through the force field. Jessica hung on tight to the little girl's hand. When she was almost there, Jessica began to feel a tingling in her body. Still she clung to the little girl. Sharp darting pains shot through her. Still Jessica refused to let go. A force knocked her back, more powerful than she'd ever felt before. She sank to the ground. She lay there gasping, while the crowd looked away.

Chapter 39

It took Sebastian days to get to Custer. His horse was weary, but he'd been forceful. Along the way he encountered deep ravines he was sure were newly created. The scope of the damage concerned him. There had been a few aftershocks, none of them too worrisome. But it seemed the closer he came to Custer, the more severe the damage.

Now, looking down the main street, he sat stunned. Most of the brick buildings had collapsed. Not one person or vehicle moved.

Tomahawk shuddered beneath him. Suddenly aware of how long he'd been riding, Sebastian dismounted. "Good boy," he told his horse, while he patted his side. Sebastian took the reins, and they continued their walk through town.

It wasn't his way to yell, but now he found himself calling out. How could an entire town be deserted? He picked his way to the end of the main road, turned left and walked the next road over. That's where he found the elderly man, who was hunched over a shopping cart and picking his way through the debris.

The man looked up as Sebastian neared. "Howdy," Sebastian said. He stopped ten feet away and watched to make sure the looter didn't have a weapon.

The man squinted at Sebastian and waited.

"I'm looking for my family. Where is everyone?"

The man turned his back and continued his meticulous examination of the pile of junk in front of him. "They're gone," he said.

"Where? A whole town?" Sebastian's gaze moved down the street where paper blew in the wind.

"They went to Rapid City. For the evacuation. Or south to get away. Or north. They all left. Nothing left here to stay for." The man cackled.

Sebastian nodded. "You're sure everyone went?" He couldn't believe his wife would leave when she knew he'd be at home, worried about him.

"There's a list," the man told him. He tipped his head toward the north. "Two blocks over and down the block. The Red Cross posted a list of everyone who was taken and moved to Rapid."

"Thanks, sir." Sebastian guided his horse away.

"There's also the list of the dead. At least those who were found and could be identified," the man called after him.

Sebastian refused to believe he'd find his family listed there. Tomahawk nickered.

He found the list of those who'd been identified as dead first. Sebastian shook his head and, without looking, moved to the second list, which identified those who'd been taken to Rapid City. He ran his finger down name after name, praying he'd find his family safe. He was rewarded. Eli Navarro. Quickly he continued his scanning and found Xavier's name. Tears filled his eyes and he wiped them away as he searched for Susan's name. Nothing. He ran his hand down the list again, slowly and carefully. Still, her name wasn't there. Reluctantly, he moved to the list of confirmed dead. Once again he took his time. When he was done he sighed. Her

258

name wasn't on either list. Unsure what this meant, he looked north. The road from Custer to Rapid City was through the Black Hills National Forest. He figured it was about forty miles.

Sebastian wiped his brow. "Come on, boy. We've got a ways to go yet."

Chapter 40

P.J. stood. It felt too confining. He stared out across the room. On the floor, the boys were looking at the picture of their mom, talking about all the things they would miss.

"P.J. will you read us bedtime stories?"

"Sure," he said absently, although he wasn't sure where the stories would come from.

Preparing to leave the earth felt weird to P.J. Their ship headed into the direction of the unknown. The wide expanse of the galaxy surrounded them.

"I'll miss peanut butter," Mack said.

P.J. laughed. "I'll miss hot chocolate with marshmallows," he said, looking down at the boys. Out of the corner of his eye an elusive being caught his attention. She was beautiful. Shrouded in light with luminescent blue skin, she stood before them. Her kind purple eyes gazed at the children gathered around. She waited for everyone to quiet before speaking. The alien had fiery orange hair. P.J.'s breath caught in his throat.

Her voice boomed, echoing off the walls. "It will be okay now. Things will be better for you and you will be safe. In a short time we will exit this ship and enter a larger one, where you will join the others we've saved. The accommodations are much more comfortable. It will be the disk that transports you to your new home." To her left, a door opened and another alien appeared.

∞-Most High Elected, you did well calming the Disposables.- ∞

∞-We must prepare to unload.-∞ She floated through the doorway and was gone.

It was then P.J. realized they hadn't moved their lips.

Chapter 41

There was nothing Johnny could do about the vomit on his shoes, like there was nothing he could do about Trisha. His heart ached.

"Who knows, maybe she can get on another ship." Wesley encouraged him. "There's bunches of them coming and going. Maybe the next one will let her on. You never know."

But Johnny was sure. He'd lost her.

The ship became more stable once they made it out of the earth's atmosphere and Johnny and the others began to breathe a bit easier. The children became weary of standing and found space to sit. Wesley and Johnny carefully walked across the room so they could look outside.

Other children moved closer to the center of the ship, as far from the windows as possible, afraid they would fall. This allowed Johnny and Wesley plenty of room to spread out and look at the stars.

"Wow! This is incredible. I wonder how long we'll be flying?" Wesley asked.

Johnny had to admit, after the funny take off, he was a bit worried about traveling the galaxy in what seemed to be an outdated model of an alien ship.

"Look!" a boy of about thirteen shouted in Johnny's ear.

Johnny looked where the child pointed. Ahead, they could see a larger space vehicle. Lights shined through the little windows around the front of the large, spherical ship.

Above them on the ceiling, once again the creature that called himself Bodha appeared. "We have almost arrived at our destination. After we join with our home place, the doors will open, and you will need to move forward out of the transport ship into the area beyond."

"I wonder if this ship is going back to earth?" Johnny questioned.

Wesley shrugged. "Don't think about it."

"What?"

"You know. Staying in this ship and returning to Earth. First of all, I told you, Trisha may have been able to get on another ship. Second, this ship will be going to another location, and there's no way you'd be able to return to her. You'd probably end up in Africa or someplace and then what?"

"I can't leave her," Johnny said.

"There's nothing more you can do."

The home spaceship grew larger and larger until Johnny and Wesley felt like ants approaching a giant's table. Johnny was getting ready to stand when the transporter docked and the room jerked. It knocked him on his butt.

"Please exit into the next room," Bodha, advised from the ceiling.

The doors across the room opened, and the children made their way out. Wesley and Johnny followed. Johnny still wasn't sure if Wesley was right. The ship would probably be going back to the Earth. But he didn't believe the aliens would be going back to Wyoming either. But what if Trisha was still on the ground waiting for him? What if he didn't go back and she didn't make it because she waited for him?

When it was only Wesley and Johnny left in the spaceship, Johnny hesitated.

"Come on," Wesley told him. "You can't go back."

"Please exit into the next room," the speaker above them said. "Please move away from the doors."

Wesley pulled on Johnny's sleeve. Ahead, the other children stood in a large white and shiny metal room.

"Please clear the door," Bodha hummed.

Johnny stepped into the white room with Wesley. The doors closed behind them.

The room had smooth, walls that rose ten feet. There was nothing else.

"Great. Now what?" Wesley said, as if reading Johnny's mind.

"I . . ." Johnny heard the hissing sound first and stopped. He turned around and around, trying to find the source. When he saw it, he froze. Several hidden vents opened above their heads and white gas filtered down the walls across the room from where they stood. Already he could see the first children nod off and fall to the ground. Children panicked around them, scrambling to find a safe place that didn't exist.

"They're gassing us!" Johnny cried. He coughed covering his mouth and nose with his sleeve.

Wesley sank to the floor, his head in his hands. "Why? Why would they do that?"

Chapter 42

The room was deserted. Gillian didn't think too much of it. All morning there'd been people coming and going. She went to lift the heavy pots of sweet potato plants onto the cart.

"Have you heard?" Hammond came up behind her.

"Heard what?" Gillian asked, wiping away a lock of red hair, sticky with sweat.

Hammond lowered his voice, even though they were alone. "An earthquake hit Los Angeles. And it's opened a huge crack in the earth. People are saying Arizona's going to have ocean front property soon."

"What? That's crazy," Gillian said.

"Yeah, a 7.8."

"How do you know?"

"My mom came to find me. She gave me a couple of snack bars. Want one?" he asked.

Grateful for the offer, Gillian took the bar and opened the package. "I've been starving. Thanks," she said.

"No problem. My mom is not part of the science crew. That means she has time to worry over me. Soon as they saw her, though, someone sent her to do a task."

They ate silently for a moment. When they were finished, they grabbed the next set of plants. The entire time, no one else appeared.

"Doesn't this seem strange?" Gillian asked sweeping an arm toward the front of the room where Professor McMullen presided all morning.

"Actually, yeah, it does. Wonder what's going on."

"Me too, but if we're worried about having enough to eat and breathe, then maybe there should be someone helping down here."

They finished loading the cart and set off for the ship.

Inside the first flap, they saw a tall, gangly man. Hammond nodded when they passed the stranger.

"Who's that?" Gillian asked.

"Bug guy," Hammond told her. "He's a bit of a weird one."

"Is he part of the colony? It seems strange to bring an exterminator."

"He's going all right. He's part of the, 'must have' group. But he's not an exterminator. He's supposed to make sure all the bugs do their jobs and don't overpower the plants. His stuff is pretty cool, really. When I first came here, I toured his lab. He's got bees, butterflies, ants and all kinds of other bugs."

Gillian turned, but the bug guy was already gone.

Inside the second flap, all was quiet. They passed through the area and were quickly in the agriculture section again. Only one other cart passed them.

Hammond looked around. "Now I'm getting angry. Where is everyone?"

They unloaded and loaded the cart again. Finally, all of the sweet potato plants were squished into the bay. With no more potatoes to carry, they switched and began to help with

266

the garden vegetables. Gillian and Hammond carried lettuce, radishes, and tomatoes into the ship.

Systems below the habitat were being checked, and as they walked through the different areas, they were sometimes drenched in water or sprayed by misters.

"Do you have any idea what time it is?" Gillian asked.

Hammond checked his cell phone. "Three."

"Now what?" Gillian looked around. They still hadn't seen the Professor and it had been, Gillian was sure, hours.

"Hey, kids," a woman called from above them on the mezzanine. "Can you hang these lights on that railing?"

Hammond caught the string of Christmas lights and with Gillian's help, strung them over the railing although, when they were done, they saw no place to plug them in and wondered what they were for.

A group of men pushed and pulled a large fan into the room and positioned it. They worked to restrain it.

"I'm sure there's stuff to do, but I don't know what," Hammond said. "I'm going to go up and see what's going on in control."

They called the elevator and then waited for it to arrive. It didn't take long.

"What about you?" Hammond asked when they entered. He pushed the button for the control room.

"I'll go with you," Gillian told him.

The door closed and the elevator rose gently.

"What are you going to miss most?" Hammond.

"Music," she said. "I'm going to miss music and movies."

"Hands down, I'm going to miss beef. No hamburgers. No steak." Hammond shook his head.

267

The elevator started to wiggle and then slowed to a stop. The light that illuminated the small compartment went out. Gillian became aware of the earth's movement.

"Earthquake," she said calmly as she sat down on the floor.

Hammond didn't answer.

Gillian lifted her hand and placed it in front of her face. She couldn't see it, even when it was so close it touched the tip of her nose.

The movement stopped. "You okay?" Gillian asked. In the dark she chewed a fingernail.

Everything was still. "Hammond!" Finally the lights flickered on. He sat hunched in the corner, his hands over his ears.

"That's why there's no way I'm staying on this planet," he said and stood. His hands punched the buttons on the keypad. "Do something! Come on! Do something!"

Gillian and Hammond were only stuck on the elevator for a few minutes before a bell rang and the car moved up.

When the elevator doors opened, they stepped into the control room. It was packed. They could barely squeeze out before the doors closed and the elevator retreated to its next port of call.

The large screen was filled with the image of the blond newscaster Gillian had seen each time she watched television. Now though, next to her head, were the images of smashed roadways and demolished buildings. "No word yet on casualties," the women announced.

Hammond pulled Gillian through the crowd and was soon standing beside his father. "Dad?"

268

Captain Young looked at the two of them, his face devoid of emotion. "Were you able to get the plants for Ship Two into the cargo bay?" his father asked.

"Yeah, but Dad, we got caught in the elevator. There was an earthquake."

"Go to your room and collect your things. You have," he looked at the computer screen in front of him on the table, "twenty-five minutes and then I want you on board the ship. Your mother should be waiting for you in the room. Tell her to pack my things and take them with her. Hurry, son. Go now, before I make my announcement. And Gillian, take your parents too. If you don't take them now, I'm not sure they'll leave their positions."

Captain Young pushed his way toward Gillian's parents. He stooped and spoke quietly to them. Gillian's mother turned to look at her. She nodded. Hammond was already making his way back to the elevator. He pushed the call button.

"I don't understand," Gillian said.

"Shhh," Hammond told her. "Don't say anything."

As the elevator doors opened, the bug man pushed by them and entered, moving all the way to the back. Hammond stepped in and held the door open. Professor McMullen came into view and he too stepped inside the elevator.

"Come on, Gillian," Hammond said.

Gillian took a step forward and then turned around. "I can't," she said. She looked at Hammond. "My parents."

"Come on girl. Get in here right now. Get in or we'll leave without you," Professor McMullen said. His voice seethed with urgency.

Another man and woman came up from behind Gillian and stepped inside the car. They held hands.

269

"We need to leave," the bug man said.

"Not yet. Wait for her parents," Hammond said.

Gillian stood on tiptoes, her eyes searching the crowd.

"Move away from the door or get out," Gillian heard the bug man say.

"Are you coming or not?" the woman asked. "Please, we need to leave."

Gillian stepped inside the elevator slowly. Hammond nodded and took his hand away.

"Finally," the bug man said.

Gillian's parents came toward them through the closing doors. Gillian reached forward and stuck her hand out even as the others tried to pull her back. She couldn't reach the door. Tears came to her eyes as she strained to stop the elevator.

At the last possible second, her father's hand jutted into the slit of the door and the doors peeled back. Bridget rushed in with Cal right behind her. Her father reached toward the panel and pushed the button to close the doors.

"Thanks for waiting for us," Bridget said.

"What about my father?" Hammond asked.

"He gave you instructions, right?" Cal asked.

Hammond nodded.

"Then do as you were told. We need to act swiftly. We may have a problem. Everyone here was interested in working on the project when it was just a scientific endeavor to get a group to Mars, but now that it has another appeal, they may not wish to be left behind."

They reached the seventh floor, and everyone, except for one man, stepped out. "I'll keep the elevator here," he said. "Get my things," he told his wife.

Everyone hurried to their rooms. "What's going on?" Gillian stood as her mother and father threw clothes into their suitcase.

"Gillian, this is not the time. Get your things and get them now. Hurry," her father said.

Only moments before her parents didn't seem to be moving. Now they were frantic. Bridget was putting all of the belongings from the bathroom into a bag. "I'll be in there to help you in a minute," she said.

Gillian never really unpacked. She grabbed her stuffed animal and zipped her bag. Seconds later, she was back in her parent's room and ready to go.

"Great," her mother said and shooed them out the door. Several other families made their way to the elevator. Soon, Gillian's family found themselves waiting in a line.

"Is the elevator here?" someone asked.

"Just went to the loading area. It'll be right back," someone else replied.

"What do we know? Has anyone heard anything?"

"All is quiet so far," the Professor said.

Gillian searched the corridor for Hammond and his mother but couldn't see them. She turned to search the area behind her. Nothing.

She heard a bell and the elevator doors opened. Several people in front crammed inside until there was no more room.

"How many?" Cal Turner asked the man who ran the elevator.

"Twenty-four," the man said. "Sheila is counting as we get off downstairs. I'll be right back for the last of you. Stay put." The bell chimed and the doors closed.

"Quit fidgeting," Bridget said to Gillian.

Gillian hoped, since she didn't see him, Hammond was already on the ship. She agonized over wishing the elevator would come faster to wishing it would wait so Hammond and his mother could join them. When she heard the bell sound, Gillian was both sad and thrilled. The doors opened and she stepped inside.

"This everyone?" Cal asked.

"Almost," the man said, giving Gillian's dad a sideways glance.

"Any problems yet?" Bridget asked.

The man shook his head. Gillian wasn't sure if there weren't any problems, or if her parents were being told not to talk about it in front of her.

The doors opened and everyone stepped into the loading area. There were still carts filled with things that hadn't made it onto the shuttle scattered around them. Gillian saw the members of the team who'd come down before them, working to push on as many carts as possible. Cal and Bridget each grabbed one, threw their belongings on top and headed toward the ship. Gillian was quick to grab one herself.

"Make sure everything is locked down," the Professor ordered. "If you don't have a place to lock it down, leave it. Anything gets loose and someone could be killed."

The other members of the team left the loading area. "We're going to do a final sweep of the ship," someone said.

"Give me your bags," the bug man said. He stuffed them into a closet, pushing and pushing on the door until it finally closed.

"Little lady, you and your mother should go upstairs and get into your seats," the man from the elevator said. "We've got this." He pointed to a spiral staircase that led up.

272

"I'm going to stay down here," Cal replied. "And wait for Captain Young."

Her parents shared a soulful look.

Bridget took Gillian's hand. "Come on."

From upstairs, everything looked so beautiful. Large trees soared to the next level. Man-made rocks rose into a miniature mountain. Bridget and Gillian pushed through the plastic doorway and then moved through a door similar to those used on submarines.

"It's time to get your suits on," a woman told Bridget and held out a spacesuit. "Hurry."

Bridget looked behind her.

"Don't worry. Everyone downstairs is putting theirs on right now. And we have plenty of seats, so they'll be fine. Worry about your daughter and get her into her suit."

Bridget and the woman helped Gillian into her suit and then led her to a large recliner. She was told to sit, then was strapped in. It wasn't until the woman left that Gillian turned her head to see Hammond sitting beside her.

"T-30," a man's voice announced.

She smiled. Hammond's smile was weak and Gillian knew he worried about his father.

"T-20."

Gillian was startled by the figure that dashed past them in his suit. Who? Gillian wondered.

"T-10."

A voice from the cockpit came over the speakers that fed to their space suits, "I need everyone in a seat and strapped in."

"T-9."

"T-8."

"We should all be proud to be a part of this amazing adventure," the voice from the cockpit spoke again.

"T-7."

"T-6."

Gillian felt the ground beneath her shake. She heard a loud groan.

"T-3."

"T-2."

"T-1."

The rattling and shaking of the ship increased and then in an instant, they were rising.

The space ship burst into the sky, pushing Gillian back against the seat of the recliner with a force like that of an amusement park ride. Soon the jerking motions stopped and it seemed as if they were gliding.

She was pleased to be able to turn her head.

Hammond found he could finally move and looked out the oval window beside his seat. Gillian leaned forward and touched Hammond on the arm.

Hammond recoiled.

"What?" she mouthed.

"I saw something," he replied.

"What?"

"I don't know," Hammond said, his eyes wide.

Chapter 43

"I don't want to worry and listen to the events unfold on the radio," Mandy said as their car careened down the deserted road south of Phoenix. "I'm scared. But I'm also proud of us. And I want to keep being proud."

"Mandy, this is going to be bad," Derek cautioned. "We're going to have to start over. Work from the ground up."

"No worries. I'm a hard worker," Jesse interjected.

"I'm not a little girl. I can hold my own," Mandy said.

"I know you're not, but you need to realize this isn't going to be peas and carrots."

"I'm aware. I'm sad, it's crazy all that we've lost, but I don't want to live every day thinking about what could have been either."

Jesse shut the window and she saw him lean back against the cab.

"Derek, I'm sort of excited. I never believed I'd leave Wyoming. And now look where we are."

Derek stared at her as if she'd grown two heads. Mandy knew she had started to change when she said goodbye to her parents and the dream of one day owning the ice cream shop.

Derek swerved, his arm muscles bulging as he tightened his grip on the steering wheel to miss a rabbit in the middle of the road.

"Are you trying to kill us?"

"No, I was trying to save that poor defenseless bunny."

Derek took the exit to Oracle, Arizona. He bumped along a dirt road. Doublewide trailers sat on the left. One was attached to a truck parked in front of a rundown building. Moments later, he stopped.

"What are we doing?"

"Taking care of business," he said as he hopped out of the truck and headed toward a bush. Jesse jumped down and followed.

Mandy dug under the seat to find Charlie's leash.

"We might as well take advantage, if we're going to be here awhile," she said to the dog. They climbed down and headed in the opposite direction.

"Where you going?" Derek asked.

"Away from you guys." Mandy heard him laughing.

She wondered what time it was. She hadn't realized how dark it had become. She looked toward the trailer. No lights were on and the few streetlights also sat dark. That's really weird she thought. "It looks like the power is out again," Mandy shouted.

Charlie barked at a high-pitched frantic level, and pulled on her leash.

Concern filled Mandy. "Derek, Derek," she screamed and ran. She let go of Charlie's leash and rushed to the clearing where she'd left them. She could barely see in front of her. She searched the sky for the moon and stars. They were there seconds before. All was black. Mandy screamed again as a beam of light flashed on and grabbed Jesse. He was lifted up and then disappeared. Next the beam caught Derek and chased him as he ran around the field.

276

"Run toward the truck," Mandy yelled, but he didn't change course. She didn't understand why he was darting back and forth and not heading to safety. Charlie barked next to her matching Mandy stride for stride as she ran trying to get closer. She searched the area for help. She stumbled and hit the ground hard. A second later, she was up and running to join her brother.

She reached Derek as the beam latched onto him. She tried to step into the light. She would go too, but the beam had a force field that wouldn't let her through. She reached for his hand, and came up empty. And then it was as if he was there, but not.

Derek mouthed something to her, but she didn't know what. Tears streamed down her face as she fell to her knees and pounded at the light beam. Already it was becoming more difficult to see him.

"Derek, no, no, you can't leave me," she cried.

He floated to a set of open doors, and disappeared from view.

When the ship left, the stars and the moon re-appeared, lighting up the night. Mandy couldn't believe it. She sobbed into Charlie's fur, as the dog quieted her furious barking down to a whine.

March 21st

Chapter 44

When Mandy woke the next morning, the sun streamed through the windows of the truck. She looked around, sad and terrified. Charlie barked and Mandy dropped to the floor. She covered her head with her hands. She didn't want to go with the aliens. She sucked in air and held her breath, hoping they didn't have the capability to find her. She waited, but nothing happened.

Charlie began scratching at the door and Mandy felt silly, Charlie needed to go to the bathroom. She rose from her hiding place and let the dog out. She had to go to the bathroom too, but there was no way she was leaving the truck. Sometime the night before, she'd decided she needed to continue with the plan. Derek wouldn't expect her to stay there. If he were able to escape, he'd look for her at the Biosphere.

Charlie bounded back, and Mandy let her in. She jumped over and looked expectantly for breakfast. Mandy grabbed a food bar from behind the seat and fed it to her.

"Sorry, this is all you get." Charlie barked and gobbled down the bar.

Mandy started the truck and headed toward the Biosphere. They'd been so close. She turned left onto a winding road. The air in the truck grew colder and she shivered. The sun disappeared behind weird fog and cloud cover. Mandy struggled to see the road in front of her. She moved to the edge of the seat and squinted. It wasn't fog, but it was thick like fog. Mandy had no idea what it was. She kept driving, hoping she wouldn't miss the building.

She drove around blind corners, down dips and back up again. Her palms were sweaty. She picked up speed going down a small hill and almost lost control. She hit the brakes. She didn't slide, so it wasn't rain on the road. She gripped the wheel tighter.

Rounding a corner, she gained speed again. She went down into a dip and then came back up only to slam on the brakes, inches from a large, locked metal gate, which blocked her entrance to safety.

"Nooooooo," she screamed, slamming her hand on the dashboard. She looked to the left and then the right. She needed to get around the fence. In the field beside her, she saw barbwire. She looked for wire cutters in the glove box of the truck, but didn't find any.

"Oh, well, I guess we have nothing to lose," she said.

Mandy backed up and angled herself on the other side of the road giving herself plenty of room to ram the fence. She wasn't sure of the logistics, and thought she might need to try it a few times before she gained enough speed to make it through. Mandy revved the engine. Charlie whined.

"You look nervous," Mandy told her. Charlie sank to the floorboards, lay down and put a paw over her eyes.

"I don't blame you. I wouldn't want to be up here either."

Mandy hit a divot in the ground, but didn't slow. She slammed into the fence. It gave way with the weight of the truck and they easily made it through.

"Yeah," she cheered. Charlie lifted her head, but didn't climb back onto the seat. Mandy continued driving toward where she thought the dome was. When she got to the edge of an embankment, she climbed out of the truck and looked around. The massive glass building sat in a crater thirty feet from her.

Mandy gasped. It was beautiful. She bit her lower lip. There would be no way to get the truck any closer and it would take several trips to pack in the food. Mandy grabbed two backpacks and filled one with food. She closed the door and locked the truck. She'd come back later for more.

She turned toward the building as a noise pierced the air. Mandy hit the ground covering her ears, and screaming in pain. She yelled for Charlie, but couldn't hear her own voice.

And that's when she knew the Yellowstone volcano had erupted.

Chapter 45

"Nine months is a long time," Gillian said. She moved around the shuttle easily now that they were no longer affected by Earth's gravity.

Hammond worked beside her, pulling the weeds already showing their heads.

"Mars is a long way away," Hammond said.

"Nine months. Isn't that funny, that's exactly how long it takes for a baby to be born. Nine months," Bridget said, "and we'll birth a new nation."

The three of them worked quietly together. They cleared another potato patch in the agricultural center.

"Hey, it's almost time for dinner. I'm cooking." Cal stood on the mezzanine and called down to the colonists who were all busy working in the mini biospheres on the shuttle.

"Good, I'm starving," Hammond said.

Chapter 46

∞

Ka's ships moved away from the Water Planet. Already it was becoming as nothing. Ka remembered the last time he'd come hunting and the brilliant lights that bespoke of civilized life. Now there was darkness. Their lights dead.

∞-Most High, you have achieved much. The holds are full.- ∞

Ka acknowledged the thoughts from the ship's commander and dismissed him.

He'd picked off the remaining disposables, one by one, finding them in their hiding places and snatching them from their world. Now they resided in the bowels of the ship – a dank and dirty place. He had no thought to how they would survive, but each time he'd raided the planet before, he'd been surprised by their resilience in making the trip to the Astral Zone.

He thought of the last beings he'd taken. He'd come across three who seemed to be fleeing. How primitive their thoughts. They were connected. That much he knew. He'd savored the hunt and then, only at the last moment, decided to take the strongest two of the species.

Omis entered his private thoughts as she came into his presence.

∞-Beloved,-∞ Omis thought. ∞-I am most enamored.-∞

Ka leaned over and placed his head beside hers. Immediately Omis's thoughts came even faster to Ka. He let them enter and linger while he remained beside her.

∞-You are Most High of the Most High. Soon you shall be a force for all of the Astral Zone to be uneasy about.-∞

Omis's thoughts were a song to Ka's being. They filled him with energy. Ka's heart-space opened wide for his precious.

∞-Will you now seek your rightful position in the council?-∞ Omis moved closer to Ka's being. Her thoughts wrapped themselves around his.

∞-Your thoughts are perfectly in alignment with mine,-∞ he transmitted.

Omis purred. ∞-Oh, how our bodies will shine!-∞

End of Book One

Acknowledgements

It takes a community to raise a child and as many people to write a novel. There are so many to thank.

Next coffee shop, Glendale, Arizona who allowed us to formulate words over months and months of Saturdays and taking their "best" table to do it all.

Austine Etcheverry would like thank her husband, Jared. Without his support, this would have never made it into print.

D. Jean Quarles would like to thank her family and the supportive community of writers who have been there every step of the way.

288

Authors

Austine Etcheverry was born in Sheridan, Wyoming. A wife and mother of two, she currently resides in Avondale, Arizona. A special education teacher, she writes women's fiction and young adult fiction. She is a lover of animals and currently shares a home with three dogs and six cats.

D. Jean Quarles was born in Minncapolis, MN. She currently resides in Alexandria Minnesota with her husband. She is the author of the women's fiction novels; *Rocky's Mountains, Fire in the Hole* and *Perception*. Her award winning short story, *The Mermaid*, was published in *Tales of a Sweltering City*.